Watson: My Life

~~

David Ruffle

Paperback ISBN 978-1-78705-272-7
ePub ISBN 978-1-78705-273-4
PDF ISBN 978-1-78705-274-1

Published in the UK by MX Publishing
335 Princess Park Manor, Royal Drive,
London, N11 3GX
www.mxpublishing.com

Cover layout and construction by
Brian Belanger

Also by David Ruffle

Sherlock Holmes and the Lyme Regis Horror
Sherlock Holmes and the Lyme Regis Horror (expanded 2nd Edition)
Sherlock Holmes and the Lyme Regis Legacy
Holmes and Watson: End Peace
Sherlock Holmes and the Lyme Regis Trials
The Abyss (A Journey with Jack the Ripper)
A Twist of Lyme
Sherlock Holmes: The Lyme Regis Trilogy (Illustrated Omnibus Edition)
Another Twist of Lyme
A Further Twist of Lyme
Holmes and Watson: An American Adventure
The Gondolier and the Russian Countess
Holmes and Watson: An Evening in Baker Street
Sherlock Holmes and the Scarborough Affair (with Gill Stammers)

For Children
Sherlock Holmes and the Missing Snowman (illustrated by Rikey Austin)

As editor and contributor
Tales from the Stranger's Room (Vol.1)
Tales from the Stranger's Room (Vol. 2)
Tales from the Stranger's Room (Vol.3)

Preface

Being seen locally as a Sherlock Holmes expert, even though it's not something I have ever claimed to be, often results in many questions aimed my way on various aspects of Holmes's life. I seem to be the 'go to' man for such enquiries. Where did Holmes retire to? When did he die? Did Holmes and Watson ever fall out? Did Holmes's hives ever produce honey? You get the idea. On occasion, I am given press cuttings about Holmes or even books which people no longer have a use for, but feel they would best enhance my Sherlock Holmes collection such as it is.

I was unprepared however for what I received recently over the shop counter; old biscuit tins! Sadly, they were devoid of biscuits or indeed any form of edible treat. The actual content was comprised of several cylinders, neatly labelled with various dates from March 1936 to July the same year. A separate piece of paper inside the last tin I opened bore the legend: Doctor John H Watson with a date of August the 23rd 1936. It was an Alice Sefton who had donated these tins to me and thought, rightly so, that the contents would be of great interest to me. She explained that her grandfather, Alfred Huntley, had, at the beginning of the twentieth century acted as an agent for the Edison Company, particularly involved with the marketing of their dictation machines. Possessed of both a literary bent and an inquisitive nature he began to prepare booklets and pamphlets based on the memoirs of those whom today we would call celebrities. His method was simplicity itself. Each of his chosen subjects would be left a dictation machine and a supply of wax cylinders. They were simply invited to talk about their lives, and once collected by Huntley, he would edit and then publish. He died in October 1936 after a short illness. Alice Sefton thought that due to the absence of any other cylinders in the possession of her family that these recordings were the last to be collected by her grandfather and that he fell ill before he could begin the task of editing Watson's words. But, are they Watson's words? It's impossible to be sure. After I had digitally formatted the tapes which certainly tidied up the sound, relieving it of the crackles and fizzes that disfigured it, I was left with a warm, strong although sometimes hesitant voice which certainly convinced me they were the words of a man in his eighties. I cannot go further than that. Perhaps like Watson, I am too timid in my inferences! Alice Sefton, two weeks later, produced some correspondence between her grandfather and Watson revealing something of Watson's humility. These I have reproduced here. Other than that, what you will read are Watson's own words, telling his story through a medium that may well have been foreign to him. Unlike Alfred Huntley I have decided against editing this account and have transcribed Watson's words exactly as they were when he spoke into Huntley's dictation machine just over eighty years ago.

David Ruffle Lyme Regis 2017

Dear Doctor Watson,

Please allow me to introduce myself, I am Alfred Huntley. I do not flatter myself that you may have heard of me, but I am tolerably well known in my field. For several years now, I have been publishing small memoirs of those people who are or have been in the public eye. This I do by making recordings of my chosen subjects discoursing on their lives which I collate, edit judiciously if need be and then produce in booklet or pamphlet form depending on their size.

I was planning to interview your old friend, Sherlock Holmes before his untimely death and you have my condolences, sir. I then thought that you would be an ideal replacement if you like. I don't mean to imply that you are in any way second-best. Tell me, would it be a project you could see yourself participating in?

I look forward very much to your reply,

Yours sincerely,
Alfred Huntley.

Dear Mr Huntley,

I thank you for your recent letter which I have to admit did intrigue, and I thank you very much for your offered condolences. I am none too sure that anyone would care to hear about the story of my life. For most people, I am known as Sherlock Holmes's friend and biographer and my life outside of that twenty years or so would have nothing to offer by way of comparative excitement. Not that I feel I haven't lived a full life, but how much of it would be of interest to the general public I cannot tell. However, in spite of my doubts and misgivings I am intrigued enough to be eager to know more.

How do we proceed?

Yours,
John H. Watson

Dear Doctor Watson,

Thank for your speedy reply. I propose to call upon you on a day you deem convenient and bring with me the simple apparatus which I am sure you will find easy to operate. Once having shown you how the system works I will leave everything with you. There will be no necessity to contact me again, bar there being a problem with the equipment, until you feel you have said all you need to say. Once you reach that point all you need to do is write me a letter to that effect and I will call and collect your full cylinders.

Yours etc,
Alfred Huntley

Dear Mr Huntley,

That all seems most satisfactory. Would you care to call at ten o' clock on the morning Wednesday 7ᵗʰ March? My housekeeper, Mrs Brownlow, makes a perfect cup of tea and sublime shortbread biscuits.

Yours,
John H. Watson

Watson: My Life

Cylinder 1

Ahem, I scarcely know where to start. Mr Huntley has given me a set of guidelines on how to set about it, but I am still beset by doubts. Where do I begin? At the very beginning? My life with Holmes? I have made some notes, let me see, where are they? Hm..er...my decision is made, I will travel back in time as it were long, long before my association with Sherlock Holmes. I...I was born in Hexham in Northumberland in the autumn of 1854. My father, Henry was a glover by profession and very well respected in the area. I suppose he did moderately well for I cannot recall having to go without anything. There was stiff competition in Hexham, it was a town widely known for its glove-making industry, although less so by the time of my birth.[1] The skills he used were the same skills that proved his downfall for his sight suffered from all the intricate close-up work he had to do. All the gloves, known as 'Hexham Tans' were made by hand.

---

[1] By 1902 the last tannery in Hexham had closed its doors.

One of the earliest memories I have is of seeing my father at work in his small, aroma-filled workshop. His gnarled yet delicate hands making a simple, running stitch with a glover's needle which had a sharpened, triangular point designed to penetrate the thin sheepskin. The gloves were destined to be mostly imported to the North of Europe, America and eventually Australia. I remember packing a pair when I sailed to Ballarat, but I get ahead of myself.

Where was I? Oh, yes. As my father's sight declined so did the gloving trade due in no small measure to the lifting of the prohibition on the importing of French gloves. The glovers of Hexham could not compete with these cheap, machine-made gloves, and by the time of my third birthday, there was only one glover left. My father had no choice but to leave off his trade in the summer of 1857, his sight damaged to the point of almost total blindness. The Watson family, which comprised my father, my mother, Mary and my elder brother, also a Henry, felt the loss of my father's trade keenly for not only did we lose our breadwinner but also our accommodation, for we lived on the premises that my father worked from, a modest yet spacious enough building on Tyne Green Road. The four of us found ourselves living with my mother's parents in Corbridge. Another modest building, but with absolutely no space to spare. I remember dark corners where spiders spun webs with impunity, the shuffling footsteps of my father as he negotiated his new surroundings and his new circumstances, the smells originating from the kitchen where my grandmother seemed to be permanently cooking. There was an endless supply of bread and cakes; she was at her happiest rooted in domesticity.

It was left to my mother to go out and earn a wage although she had no skills as such to fall back on in the wide world. Once she had finished her schooling she was expected to go into service or become part of the weaving industry that was so prominent in Corbridge. Instead, she had met my father at a church picnic which had taken place near the Roman remains to the east of the town. Until such time as they were married she scarcely left the house, the house that now we lived in. In very cramped conditions. It's odd how in the re-telling of the early part of my life how some details have remained etched in my brain and others less so. I can now barely recall even how my father and mother looked. I picture him as a large man whose presence filled the house, yet who appeared so small when hunched over his work-desk for long, long hours. I have no photographs to aid my memory save for one of my brother, and I do not know which one of us took after my father in looks.

My mother was always being called 'bonny lass' by my grandmother, but whether that was an indication of her prettiness or just a form of nickname I do not know. My grandmother remains only as a disembodied voice. As for my grandfather, nothing remains at all. As far as I can recall, I had no contact of any kind with him although we shared the same house. Er…I have lost track again. Where the deuce was I? Hmm, work…mother...yes. My mother earned her wages by cleaning at various homes in the town, something I suspect she hated, but no doubt would have seen it as her duty to enable her to provide for her family. In the early years of my childhood she became less of a presence, certainly less detectable in my memory. I catch fleeting glimpses of her in the recesses of my mind; hurrying, always hurrying.

I have no yardstick to measure my childhood in terms of happiness. We survived, we ate tolerably well. I do remember in very fine detail coming across some children's books stashed in the outhouse and being fascinated by them; these were adventures and tales of lands I would possibly never see and children such as myself doing things I might never do. When I first came across them I had not yet learned to read beyond some very basic words. Henry my brother refused all my entreaties that he should read them to me, 'books are for girls' he said. That is something that has always stayed with me. It was only when I went to the only available school in Corbridge and learned my ABC that I could fully appreciate my literary treasures; richly illustrated histories of the Kings and Queens of England, the battles, the squabbles and fights for succession. There must have been a certain amount of judicious editing for I cannot recall too many details on the various grisly ends that some came to. It was enough for a child to know that Edward II had been murdered at Berkeley Castle without being informed of the horrific manner of his murder.

Books were my boon companions not that they were in any way easy to obtain. The school had a very small collection and being the new boy, I was often last in line when it came to the doling out of those eagerly anticipated volumes. Ha-ha, I remember now that the queue was made up almost entirely of girls apart from a certain John Henry Watson. The other boys in the school sided with my brother and his declared views on the soppy reading of books. 'Books are for girls' he told me often. All the same, I often saw a look of jealousy on their faces when I had a book under my arm after eventually gaining a place at the head of the queue. Did I imagine myself as any of the people I read about? Certainly, not the kings, maybe with the honourable exception of Richard the Lionheart[2] and even then, only because of his connection, however fleeting, with Robin Hood. Oh, he was my hero all right. I made myself a flimsy bow and arrow which looked the part, but when it came to firing arrows was redundant. Still, my imagination accounted for the loosening of the arrows, often into imagined distant targets, but more

---

[2] Richard the First, of England.

often Norman soldiers in the command of the Sheriff of Nottingham. I read and re-read the tales of Robin and his merry men although having said that I did have my reservations about Maid Marian; as a mere girl, she had no place with the outlaws of Sherwood Forest. I was prepared to overlook her presence as long as she didn't slow down the action too much and Normans, tax collectors and King John's lackeys bit the dust.

You may be wondering what part my brother played in these early days of play and learning. Mostly, none. We did not play together, he had his own friends being three years older. I would say that we fought, but to call it fighting would not do our actual relationship any kind of service. He was a bully who would seek to humiliate me as often as he could although even that he would tire of and turn to the strategy of just simply ignoring me. Sadly, this kind of behaviour carried on into his adult years, sad to say we never forged a bond that other siblings have. Er...I will return to this later if this is to be a Cromwellian[3] 'warts and all' story.

When I was just eight years old my mother fell gravely ill. A silence hung over the house, a deathly silence. Any semblance of a normal life was in abatement. She lingered for a week or two before finally succumbing, worn out from the battle. The cause of death was deemed to be English cholera and a further twenty were carried off locally over the next few weeks. Given the conditions we lived in, with mould an ever present in the house and walls that seemed to be permanently bedecked with moisture, it was a miracle that none of us also contracted the disease although the family next door was to lose both their children. And...there we were...both my brother and I, motherless. She-she was just thirty-two years old. My

---

[3] Oliver Cromwell, Lord Protector insisted his portrait be painted 'warts and all'.

father could not work and in spite of my grandmother taking over some of my mother's cleaning duties, times became harder, food on the table scarcer. The solution was the obvious one; Henry would have to cease his schooling and obtain work. There was a textile mill on the southern edge of the town that provided many Corbridge families with their income, wretched work though it may have been.

Once again, my memory is lacking because I cannot recall how Henry felt about this change in his circumstances. He may have felt aggrieved. He may have thought it to be his familial duty, but knowing my brother as I did, I cannot believe that was the case unless I am impugning him and his memory. And that is quite a possibility. The few shillings a week he would have earned for his long eleven or twelve hours a day must have helped our day-to-day existence. I have a vivid remembrance from that time, wondering whether it would be my fate also to be plunged into the world of child labour. The world of childish literature had fired my imagination and my mind was set on adventure and travelling to far-flung exotic locations.

Amusing to think of it when I sit here as an old man, older indeed than any of my family managed. Well, life surprised me often and the mere fact that I am sitting here speaking into this machine proves that it can still surprise me. Within two years my brother and I were destined to lose our grandparents and our father. My father never recovered from losing his Mary and you could say, were you of a romantic bent, that he hastened his own death to be with her. As for my grandparents, they simply came to the end of their tether, not by any means uncommon in those days. With the death of my father perhaps they felt their duty was done or perhaps I am guilty of an old man's romancing the past.

My brother had attached himself to the family of one of the mill supervisors through a fondness for that man's daughter. He was taken in by them; as far as I am aware he made no such appeal for a home for his younger brother. My education was at a critical juncture; I was well thought of at school and was spoken of in glowing terms by all the teachers. My grades were uniformly excellent across the board, due I think in no small part, to my incessant reading. My thirst for knowledge was an all-abiding thing for me, my motivation. My immediate concern was where I would be living. In a close-knit working community, there was never a lack of solidarity, everyone looked out for everyone else.

It was decided, by whom I was never quite sure, that I would be housed with the Griffiths' family of whom I knew next to nothing. I suppose I was dimly aware of the existence of a Thomas Griffiths who attended the local school although without much distinction I believed. He was a little older than me with a sister who was exactly my age...to the day, almost to the hour! Her name was Lily. She was, what we called in those days a tomboy and maybe still do, I appear to be out of step with modern jargon. I know and would be the first to agree that language has to evolve with each passing generation, but some of the expressions leave me positively baffled and bemused. Perhaps there came a time in my life when I began to resist all change. Whether that was a sign that I had become entirely comfortable with my life or just that I had become set in my ways, I am not sure.

And now I have lost my thread. Ah, yes. Lily. Lily Griffiths. A tomboy was the term; she took part in all the boys' activities. A more skilled tree-climber than any of us, a deadly shot with a catapult and guaranteed to win any fist fight. But underneath it all there was a tender streak which betrayed her burgeoning femininity. She immediately became my best friend and in spite of her popularity with all her peers, I hoped I became something similar to her, if not an actual best friend then certainly one of her inner circle. I awarded her one of the highest accolades possible at that time; in my imagination, she became the fair Maid Marian. For those familiar with my chronicles of Sherlock Holmes, you could say for me she was THE woman or more properly THE girl. Not that there was any romance, we were far too young, unless it were the chivalrous, knightly love of yesteryear where the Lady Lily Griffiths would wear the colours of Sir John Watson thereby signalling the betrothal of them to each other.

Such was my life then. A life of studying hard and also giving free rein to my imagination. It may seem to you the listener...I mean the reader, that life had suddenly become idyllic for me, but it isn't really how it was, or indeed how it felt. I had lost my father, mother, grandfather, grandmother and my brother was alienated from me. To all intents and purposes, I had no family. My father's parents were unknown to me, I had never met them nor received any communication from them. I did not know where they were or even if they were still alive. All I knew, or thought I knew, was that there had been a total estrangement between my father and his family. On whose fault, the blame lie I had no idea nor the reasons behind this exile. My brother, on the occasions he deigned to speak to me, developed many theories that largely relied on scandal and/or criminal deeds to explain it away. Most of these theories went over my young head, fortunately!

At school, there was talk of scholarships, public schools and the like for me. The very idea of being sent away to public school appalled me. I had gleaned a little of life at such institutions through the books I had read, many of which seemed to be fixated on the merry and healthy life at schools such as Eton and Harrow where, if the stories were to be believed, the days were full of sunshine, cricket, rugger and all manner of jolly japes. I prided myself on the fact I had become a discerning reader and saw through these happy schooldays to the reality of discipline, a rigorous routine and homesickness. Did I consider the house I now lived in with the Griffiths' family, home? Frankly, yes. They had been good enough to take me in when it would have been far simpler to look the other way and let someone else do their duty. I have to say they were in a better position than most, certainly financially, to take in, clothe and feed a lost waif. Josiah Griffiths was a doctor and ex-army surgeon who was looked on kindly by all who knew him as far as my young eyes could see.

He conducted his surgery from home and I remember being fascinated by the streams of people who tramped through the house with their grimaces of pain often superseded by smiles of relief as they exited the house. I would often enter the hallowed grounds of his surgery at the end of the day to watch him clean up and put everything in its proper place ready to receive his first patient at nine o' clock in the morning. The bookcase naturally held a fascination for me with their banks of leather and cloth-bound medical volumes. I was allowed occasionally to take a volume out and flick through its pages assuming the content did not contain anything that could be construed as inappropriate for my tender years.

The first Christmas I was there Dr Griffiths presented me with a model skeleton, unfortunately not life-size, with a full array of working organs which could be extricated and returned to their skeletal home. For a few weeks, afterwards I was questioned as to the names of bodily parts and organs and where they belonged in the body. This only stopped when Dr Griffiths realised he was no longer going to trip me up with his questioning. In a novel, this would be the eureka moment when the hero decides in an instant that this is now his vocation. Well...this is no novel...I am no hero and there was no eureka moment accompanied by lightning strikes, thunderbolts or heavenly choirs! The very notion of doctoring had no appeal for me whatsoever. If anything, I was more taken with the life of a soldier, patrolling the limits of the British Empire putting down colonial revolutions, fighting manfully against the beastly natives.

If I had known then of the true horrors of war I would have perhaps been happier as a provincial clock maker whose only worry would be whether his clocks would chime. At fourteen, my brother ran away from the house he lived in with the supervisor's family. It was said in the town that not being particularly enamoured of Henry, the family would have been more than happy to never clap eyes on him again, but for the small matter of their daughter absconding with him! The hue and cry did not exactly reach fever pitch for they were found a day later in a barn on the outskirts of the town; cold, wet, bedraggled and you would think ashamed, but not my brother, oh no. I cannot speak for the girl. In fact, her name eludes me. Retribution was not as severe as it could have been although Henry's somewhat comfortable existence came to a swift end. The workhouse became his new home and his shifts at the mill, longer and harder. I visited him, but I was turned away.

In spite of our fractious relationship I was bitterly upset by this latest snub and our rift grew wider still. To all intents and purposes, I had no family. I may have repeated myself there, there is no way for me to check what I have already said and while my long-term memory functions well, not so my short-term. Much as I appreciated Josiah and Irene Griffiths taking me into their home I did not and would not think of them as family in spite of the kindness they had shown to me. The future was a closed book to me for I had no idea what direction it would take me in. The only certain thing was that my education would continue in one form or another. I was ahead of the rest of the school in English, comprehension, history and all the sciences. I had a hunger for learning coupled with a most inquisitive nature. The immediate concern as I approached my twelfth birthday was exactly where my further education would take place. The local education board was pressing for my enrolment into Newcastle grammar school as a boarder and as my legal guardian it would be down to Josiah Griffiths to make the final decision. However, things were about to change dramatically.

Cylinder 2

An early morning visitor altered my way of life completely. He announced himself as James Watson, my uncle. An uncle I had never seen nor even heard of. Odd the things you remember, but I can still almost taste his cologne. It laid heavy in the air and seemed to both precede and follow him with every step he took. He took a cursory look at me before retiring to Josiah Griffith's study. I stood outside the door, straining to catch anything of the conversation within. Lily came to join me and she suggested the panelling in the dining room might yield more in the way of eavesdropping fruit. That was not the case. We were not in the dark for long however.

The study door was opened, and my uncle invited me inside. Lily took a step towards the door, but her father ordered her away in no uncertain terms. Poor Lily. She did suffer so well. My fate, which was how I saw it, was settled in minutes. It had been decided with of course no consultation with me that I was now to live with my Uncle James. This man was a stranger; I didn't even know where he lived yet within minutes I was to be packing my bags and leaving what had become my home to begin a new life elsewhere without even knowing where that elsewhere was.

My newly acquired uncle informed me that my brother would not be accompanying us. He has made his decisions in life already he told me and he should be left to go his own way. He did, however, allow me to visit the workhouse where Henry still lived to enable me to say my goodbye. It was the most perfunctory of farewells, my brother displaying no emotion at my going and change in circumstances. Although we had never really bonded as siblings even when young I did wonder how this antipathy had arisen, for my part I would have been glad, and had been in the past, to offer the olive branch, but my efforts were rejected many times over.

It was with a heavy heart I boarded a train heading south, away from all I had ever known. This parting was sweetened somewhat by Lily's large, beaming smile as she waved from the platform. Would I ever see her again? The beginning of my journey south was interminable made even more so by my uncle's failure to communicate with me in any meaningful way. Once we had changed trains at Carlisle station, he settled back in his seat to sleep. Irene Griffiths had packed two sandwiches for me plus some homemade currant biscuits. I devoured those speedily and tiring of the scenery, I fished a book out of my bag, but soon the dwindling daylight made it well-nigh impossible to see the print and I too gave in to sleep.

I knew nothing more until I awoke with a raging thirst as we entered Euston station. The signs meant nothing to me at that time, but I was aware of the vastness of the station which was impossibly busy even at that late time of day. 'London' said my uncle. 'Yes, I know,' I replied, not caring whether or not my answer seemed rude or disrespectful. I was determined to show I was not some country bumpkin, but an intelligent, well-read child. But of course, he knew that, it's why he had taken me away as I was to learn very shortly.

I had not thought of that journey to London for many, many years. Odd how the emotions I feel now are exactly how I felt then. Telling my story like this plunges me back into my past so it becomes something tangible. I almost feel twelve again, but the question is…would I want to be? Idle, useless thoughts. My life has been what it was and is for better and for worse. It is unchanging and unchangeable. But still I can't help dwelling on what might have been at various points in my life, it is no doubt a symptom of old age that the past is all there is to look forward to.

But once more, I digress, but I am sure that Mr Huntley will be severe with his editing. I was familiar with London with the limited familiarity that reading can give one, but the sudden shock of finding myself in such a city, teeming with life, was a shock to my system. The noise hit me first before we had even left the station; my ears were assaulted in every imaginable way. The hissing of steam from the engines, the shouts and whistles of the porters, the clatter of trolleys laden with luggage rolling across the concourse. It was new, even frightening, but also tremendously exciting. And tiring. I was so tired, I remember it well. I could barely clamber into the cab that my uncle hailed and once inside promptly fell asleep in spite of the deep sleep I had succumbed to in the train.

When I awoke, I was being led into the darkness of an imposing looking villa. My memory is playing me false of course for I only knew how imposing it looked on closer scrutiny in the light of the following day. I was handed over to the care of a housekeeper introduced to me as Mrs Chinneck who proceeded to take this sleepy boy in hand and before too much time had elapsed I found myself in the most comfortable bed I had ever seen or experienced. It will come as no surprise to anyone who has ever known me that I surrendered to the arms of Morpheus once more. Which is what I must do now. I dreamt of my twelve-year-old self last night, yet with subtle differences; for instance, a young Sherlock Holmes was my new neighbour and the villa had somehow become 221b Baker Street. Mrs Chinneck had taken the place of dear Mrs Hudson and was urging me to eat my breakfast before venturing out to fight crime. 'It's the same advice I give to all growing boys,' she was saying. I pointed out that Holmes was not eating his breakfast and was told in no uncertain terms that 'good boys don't tell tales.' Then Lily walked in and announced that 'the game was afoot.' Who can fathom the workings of the human mind? Who can gauge how dreams are formed?

The truth was that Mrs Chinneck had no need of urging me to eat that first breakfast for it was a meal to set before a king. Of my uncle, there was no sign. 'Gone out for his constitutional,' I was told. I was so full of questions that I scarcely knew where to begin and was not best pleased that the majority of those questions would remain unanswered for a while at least. I did learn that I was now in Forest Hill in the southeast of London. The villa lay in Manor Mount, a fairly short street with many such fine villas. The house still stands now and looks just as grand. Three years ago, I was intrigued to read that Dieter Bonhoeffer the well-known German dissident was living in the house while he took up residence as the pastor of the German Lutheran church in Sydenham.

Once breakfast was over I went back to my room to dress. The clothes I had worn on my journey to London were gone, but in the wardrobe and chest of drawers I found a complete set of clothes; shirts, collars, ties, Norfolk jackets, shoes, boots, suits. I selected items at random and raced back down the stairs. My uncle had now returned and he took me into his study. The room was lined with books although all of them looked pristine. I was prepared to wager that the vast majority of them remained unread. This appeared to be a collection for show, to impress rather than a library to be explored for hidden gems. The previously quiet, non-communicative man now opened up to me. He had taken it upon himself to play a hand, a guiding hand in my education and upbringing after he had heard several glowing reports about my appetite for learning. I heard more about our family history going back several generations. Sibling rivalries and falling-outs had blighted the generations of the Watson family it seemed. My uncle too had been rescued shall we say, by an uncle of his own and through careful nurturing had risen to be a success in the world. He was, he explained, a city merchant who traded in stocks, shares and commodities. He was the head of his own small company and presided over a staff of five. Imports, exports, all was grist to his mill. He had no son of his own to leave his business to and after my education was complete the inference was that I would become the new lynchpin.

However, much I was in the dark still about my future career, I did not see myself as a city man in any shape or form. It all sounded deadly dull to me. I was twelve though and had little or no choice in the proceedings. A school had been selected for me of course and it was a famous one although unknown to me at the time. It was St Paul's, one of the nine great public schools in the country, founded in 1509. The prospect hardly thrilled me even though the announcement was tempered by the fact I was not to be a boarder; I would be travelling each day during term to Cheapside where the school was situated. I did have a week's grace before that fateful first day of term arrived, plenty of time to explore my new surroundings. Left to my own devices I walked endlessly throughout Forest Hill, Lewisham and venturing as far as Blackheath.

Although there were elements of the countryside and the rural still visible, much of the area I came to know was built-up with much expansion to be seen. Was I lonely? Yes, but I had imagination which made up for any lack of friendship and certainly helped me cope with my new life. Perhaps I only think of myself as being lonely with the benefit of hindsight.

I was fascinated by London even if I was only getting to know its south-eastern suburbs. The villages of the area, for that is what they still were, were rapidly being linked together. New roads being built, whole streets rising from nowhere, commerce encroaching where once there were farms. I was overwhelmed by the noise, the smells that marked out all these building sites. The ground was being swallowed whole by a demanding population. In spite of the numerous pairs of boots and shoes that filled the bottom of my wardrobe it was decreed that none were suitable for the approaching visit to church so feeling rather grown-up I was despatched to Campion's shoe shop on the High Street with a sum of money that Mrs Chinneck pressed into my palm with a set of vague instructions as to what pair would be suitable for such occasions. The aroma of leather was overpowering and has never left me. I swear I can smell it still. The staff took pity on this poor boy and were very patient. Eventually, I walked out of the door clutching a pair of highly-polished black shoes. I was not so much pleased at that as the fact I had money left over and Mrs Chinneck was very clear that should be there any money left over then it was mine to spend as I wished. The exact sum I cannot recall, but I do recall it meant I could buy a slim book which was a concise, but very informative history of the British army and a map of the world to hang on my wall. The few pennies I had left over after those purchases were handed over the counter at the confectioners in return for a bag of humbugs.

My family would be best described as God-fearing folk rather than church-attending folk. The same was true of Josiah Griffiths and his family, but James Watson was of a different ilk altogether as was witnessed by our evening Bible readings. Attendance was compulsory and the 'family' was also required to be present at St Bartholomew's Church on Westwood Hill[4] twice on a Sunday. At eight o' clock every Sunday morning my uncle, Mrs Chinneck and I would depart the house in our Sunday best, clamber into my uncle's carriage and arrive at the church at eight-thirty on the dot. My uncle was a most punctual man and woe betide if either of us kept him waiting. At ten o'clock we would begin the return journey. Four hours later we would begin the same routine. It is little wonder I held religious services in such low regard in later life; there was no attempt by my uncle to teach faith in any tangible way. For him it was enough to attend church and to read the Bible daily.

Our evening Bible readings was just that: reading. The passages we read were not interpreted or enlarged upon in any way. For many years afterwards, I could if required recite vast chunks of Scripture, but with no idea of the message behind any of it. I already knew that there would be some form of religious assembly to start each day at St Paul's school. I was not looking forward to it, any of it. All too soon, my week's grace was over and the learning had to begin. It was with the heaviest of hearts that I arose on the following Monday morning at the unearthly time of six o'clock to eat a hurried breakfast and depart for school. There was no mollycoddling of any sort; I had the address of the school and the name of my form master to report to, a Mr Tomkinson, and that was it. My uncle had prepared a list of train times into the city together with a rail pass, and also a map of where to find

---

[4] Painted by Camille Pissarro in his work, 'The Avenue'.

Cheapside so I would not disgrace myself and pound the streets of the city in vain. Mrs Chinneck slipped some money into my pocket, 'for the tuck shop,' she said. The journey was no more than seven miles all told, but for me it seemed like an eternity. The carriage was crowded and I felt I could hardly breathe. I was hemmed into a corner, my satchel with paper, pencils and a fountain pen inside, perched precariously on my lap. Once at London Bridge station we were all disgorged into the outside world in an avalanche of humankind pouring forth into the streets. Once I had consulted my map and got my bearings I felt happier, but only to a degree. It was just a walk of a few minutes to Cheapside and with a backward glance at the hustle and bustle of London I entered the school although at that precise moment it felt more like a Roman arena with lions licking their lips in anticipation of the arrival of the Christians.

I felt hopelessly out of place, the weight of history which pervaded the building convinced me that I would be a failure; the country yokel whose shortcomings were about to be cruelly exposed. I asked at least seven boys where I could find Mr Tomkinson and was greeted with ribald laughter each time. Eventually, a boy who I learned later rejoiced in the name Alfred Great kindly showed me the way to Mr Tomkinson's study. I had arrived. I was given a lecture on the traditions of the school that I was expected to uphold and the standard of behaviour expected from all pupils both within the confines of the school and the world beyond it. I was blessed it seems to have an education at all intoned Mr Tomkinson for it was a fact that a third of all the children in the country did not attend a school of any sort. I didn't feel blessed I have to say. I was also provided with yet another map, this one being of the school and a table of punishments that I would be liable to for various transgressions. Spare the rod and spoil the child was the motto of those days when it came to educating the privileged few.

I was designated an Oppidan, which was a term more freely used at Eton than other schools; it merely reflected the fact that I lived outside the school and my tuition was paid for by my family, namely my uncle of course. I was spared therefore the perceived horrors of fagging for the elder boys.

However, life at St Paul's would turn out to be exhilarating and stimulating. The guiding forces of the boys were education, sports, and morals, though not always in that order, and independence of thought and a questioning outlook were encouraged. I blossomed as a result of the progressive thinkers at the school who had turned away from the religion-based curriculum to a more suitable education for young gentlemen with the emphasis not only on moral guidance and sport, but also all branches of the sciences.

But on that first day everything was an unknown quantity and by the time Mr Tomkinson had finished with me I was straining at the leash to get to my classroom for my baptism of fire. Before I could do that, and as I heard the strains of morning assembly dying away, there was one more task to perform; to meet the headmaster. The term high master was used instead of headmaster and the high master for all my time there was Herbert Kynaston. He was a renowned Latin scholar already and everyone at the school was expected to memorise all his works for recitation at any given moment. My contact with him was minimal, but I found him to be a kindly soul with a gentle, paternal manner. He addressed few words to me other than to mark my progress within the rugby team.

St Paul's indulged in all the popular sports of the day with the emphasis being on gentlemanly sports such as cricket and of course, rugby. The ex-public-school boy was expected to have a well-rounded character, impeccable manners and enviable personal qualities. Further, having led a team on the games field it was assumed that he could lead a regiment on the battlefield. According to one observer, public schools created men who would be 'acceptable at a dance and invaluable in a shipwreck!' So, in the space of sixty years, what had been an embarrassment to public school headmasters became their pride – games and athletic pursuits.

But I fear I have jumped ahead once more. How difficult this is. I find my mind going off at a tangent constantly. But then, that is true of my life as a whole these days. My memories of these early schooldays are quite trustworthy whereas if you were to ask me what I did this time last week I would struggle. Truth be told though I would be able to work it out as most days follow the same pattern; the morning papers are delivered, I read them over breakfast followed by a morning constitutional and the rest of the day is usually spent in going over my notes of over seventy cases with Holmes, but no longer with the notion of publishing them.

I decided nine years ago that my literary career, if it can be called that, was over. There was a ritualistic bent to so much of school life. I could imagine that in so many ways that nothing had ever changed for centuries. When entering the school, we were supposed to intone the school's motto: *Fide Et Literis*-By Faith and By Learning. Dean Colet who had founded the school and was Dean of St Paul's Cathedral although Colet was an outspoken critic of the powerful and worldly Church of his day, a friend of Erasmus and Sir Thomas More. Erasmus wrote textbooks for the school and St Paul's was the first English school to teach Greek, reflecting the humanist interests of the founder. Colet distrusted the Church as a managing body for his school, declaring that he "found the least corruption" in married laymen. For this reason, Colet assigned the management of the school and its revenues to the Mercers' Company, the premier livery company in the City of London, with which his father had been associated. Even now, the Mercers' Company still forms the major part of the governing body. One of St Paul's early headmasters was Richard Mulcaster, famous for writing two influential treatises on education (Positions, in 1581, and Elementarie in 1582). His description in Positions of "footeball" as a refereed team sport is the earliest reference to organised modern football. For this description and his enthusiasm for the sport he is considered the father of modern football. That is of course Association Football or soccer not rugby football.

Anyone who has ever known me will know of my preference for rugby; in fact, I have only ever attended two soccer matches both of which are permanently erased from my memory, probably rightly so. Originally, the school provided education for 153 children of all nations and countries indifferently, primarily in literature and etiquette. The number 153 has long been associated with the miraculous draught of fishes recorded in St John's Gospel, and for several generations Foundation Scholars have been given the option of wearing an emblem of a silver fish. St Paul's was the largest school in England at its foundation, and its high master had a salary of thirteen shillings and sixpence weekly, which was double that of the contemporary headmaster of Eton College. The scholars were not required to make any payment, although they were required to be literate and had to pay for their own wax candles, which at that time were an expensive commodity. Incidentally, the school moved to a new building in Hammersmith where the system of street numbering was being changed so whether by accident or design St Paul's new address was 153 Hammersmith Road.

Cylinder 3

I really must make a note of where I am at the completion of each cylinder for I have no method of playing the recordings back. Let me think...oh yes...all this wealth of history and tradition weighed down on the pupils so that we became part of the fabric of the place, part of the conventions it was founded upon. We became the institution as much as the school itself. It was not however a weight which crushed us with huge burdens of expectation. For me personally, coming from the background I had, it was a heartening and motivational experience in spite of my initial misgivings as to how I would fare in such an environment. The building itself was a thing of beauty to me although damnably difficult as a newcomer to negotiate.

Unknown to me at the time, but there was a growing awareness that architecture is required to perform a number of functions in any society. Buildings have both a rhetorical and regulatory as well as a purely functional purpose. They are intended to control behaviour and shape ideas; to exert influence and express identity. The Cheapside building certainly did that admirably.

The curriculum, which was in the process of changing rapidly, still favoured the classics hence learning Latin and Greek was still deemed to be essential for those who wished to enter university. Of course, a school like St Paul's would quite reasonably expect all its pupils to go on to university, at least those of us who intended to work for a living.

As I progressed in the school, the need for the classics became less of a requirement as the twin ideals of science and sport took hold. Athleticism was believed to be vital for our health and moral well-being. If we were encouraged to be manly, energetic, and enthusiastic at their games the idea was that we would be trained to become healthy and ingenuous throughout our whole school life; failing this course, there will arise an unmanly precocity in self-indulgence, betting, smoking and drinking.

I can certainly lay claim to being manly, energetic and enthusiastic at games, but perhaps it is wise of me not to dwell on self-indulgence, betting, smoking and drinking! I settled into school life quickly and to my surprise, easily. I was diligent and showed the necessary respect for the teaching staff. I made friends who remained friends for many years. It was contrary to my expectations for I had imagined a harsh, cruel regime. Oh, there was discipline of course; I can hear now the swish of the cane and the biting feel of it on my backside. Even the most studious of pupils could be as prone as any of us to committing the odd misdemeanour and incurring the wrath of various masters. Without exception, we saw this discipline as just and indeed, character forming. I am not by any means an advocate of cruelty, but a deserved punishment meted out fairly is just and proper. Perhaps these views are outdated now, but I stand by them.

The daily journey to the school from Forest Hill would never feel like a chore. If I may use the phrase, it became akin to a voyage of discovery. I spent my time studying my fellow passengers, trying to guess how their home lives were, what they did for employment. Funny to think of it now because without knowing it, I was employing Sherlock Holmes's methods. Of course, I had no clue as to whether my deductions had any basis in fact, but it allowed a normally mundane train journey to pass quicker.

My uncle was pleased with my progress during those first few months. Not that he said too much about it to me other than brief pats on the head and a hurried well-done. My aptitude was leaned heavily in favour of the sciences; biology, physics and chemistry I found fascinating subjects. It was, I think, during that first year that I decided that I wanted to become a doctor. There was no great flash of inspiration that brought me to that point.

Damn, I think I have said that before. I have no way of checking what has gone on to the first cylinder with no means of playing it back. And I am sure I have said that before too. I am none too sure I wish to hear my own voice thrown back at me on a machine. I digress, but I am sure Mr Huntley will edit this floundering of mine.

My decision meant I had to apply myself even harder with the years of training ahead. I was single-minded enough in those days to know that I could see it through come what may. Even so, I made sure that there was time to apply myself on the sports field also. The St Paul's rugby football team had only recently been formed, and one problem we constantly had was the dearth of opposition. We did play occasional matches against other schools, but more often than not we would be pitched against scratch sides from various London clubs. Chief amongst these was Blackheath for we shared their ground and facilities such as they were. Their first team was far too strong for us, but we put up battling displays against their more junior side. Thus, began my association with the famous Blackheath club, an association I still maintain in my honorary position of Life President.

My closest friends at school were Edward Fothergill and James Tawton; we shared ambitions and an appreciation of sport. We were also very good at devising pranks. Pranks in general were accepted as par for the course at St Paul's just as long as there was no danger to life or limb and things didn't get out of hand. Even the masters were not above joining in with the spirit of it although I am sure none would ever have owned up to it. Hauling one of the master's bicycles into a tree was deemed to be going just a bit too far and the punishment although slight, was certainly applied enthusiastically.

In this way, I stumbled through my school years. Not the best scholar, but far from the worst. I think it could be fair to say that any academic ability I displayed while at Hexham School had evaporated a little at St Paul's. I did enough, just enough, to be able to feel confident that I could succeed in my chosen profession. University was the next step for me, but as it turned out there was another step to take first, one that some found surprising, even odd.

I decided to put everything in abeyance as far as education and career was concerned and take myself off to Australia for what I imagined would be just a year. My uncle voiced no objections; he was still a little upset that I had decided against joining forces with him in his business empire. After that blow, I don't suppose he cared what I did as long as I was not in his hair. However, I remained eternally grateful to him for the opportunity he carved out for me. My place was reserved at the University of London the autumn of 1873 much to the chagrin of their board and my masters at St Paul's who would rather my education moved speedily on. I had long been giving thought to a year away from studies where I could experience life before life made its mark on me.

One of the most exciting books I had ever read at that point in my life had at its core, the Eureka Rebellion[5] that took place in far off Ballarat[6] in Australia, when miners and the army fought a pitched battle. The novel romanticised the whole affair, but I read it many times and was inspired and saddened by the events which unfolded. Therefore, my destination had to be Ballarat, for perhaps it may be said, the shallowest of reasons and so, I made my plans. I have even further reason to be grateful to my uncle for he was willing to fund my trip with the proviso that as soon as I disembarked in Australia than I was to stand on my own two feet and find for myself gainful employment. I delayed my venture for a few months owing to my friend Edward's announcement that his father was to be the medic on the steam ship Hellespont which was sailing to Melbourne in the summer of 1872. No, sorry, it was James's father, Doctor Tawton. Of course, how could I have forgotten that? Tawton was quite happy to have me assist him in any capacity I could during the voyage.

There was to be a very small remuneration for my efforts, although my wages would mostly be the experience and insight I would gain from observation of his working practices and techniques. Prior to joining the ship at Liverpool, I travelled up to Hexham to visit my brother and to Corbridge to see the Griffiths family. Henry was no longer in the workhouse and was employed in a local brickworks. He had fallen in with a local widow whose name, if indeed I ever knew it, escapes me. All I remember is that she was a

---

[5] The only armed rebellion in Australian history.

[6]Ballarat is arguably the most significant Victorian era gold rush boomtown in Australia.

coarse woman who relied on alcohol to get through her days. I had only been there a few hours before she made a most improper suggestion to me that shocked me profoundly. I was in a dilemma as to whether inform Henry or not. In the end, I decided he had a right to know. I was naïve enough to think he would care, but his reaction saddened me for he merely laughed and cursed that I should have taken up on her offer; others had he said. After that incident, I avoided him until my day of departure when we were entirely civil with another and I realised that for all his faults and yes, mine too, he was my brother and the bond of love, deep down though it may be, could not easily be broken.

My reunion with the Griffiths family was a very happy one indeed; Josiah and Irene who had known only a child were now presented with the sight of a confident young man. Thomas was away at university in Edinburgh studying medicine and intent on following in his father's footsteps. Lily, my Maid Marian of old, had done very well for herself and with a reasonable education behind her, certainly for the time, had taken on the duties as a junior teacher at Carlisle Girl's school. Not only that, but the tomboy of six years previously had become a beautiful, assured young woman. Still, for all the wonderful exterior, I had no doubts she could still climb a tree better than most, was still supremely skilled with a catapult and I was, even six years on, not prepared to engage in a fist fight with her! I was entranced by her, so much so that I almost took the step of asking her to accompany me to the other side of the world. Of course, I didn't although we made vague promises to meet just as soon as I returned. Did I love her? Certainly, on some level. Romantic love? Well, possibly, more than possible on my part and who knows? Hers as well. But those things were not mentioned or discussed and when next we met our lives were very different indeed.

To say I was not looking forward to the voyage would be a miracle of understatement. I had no experience whatsoever of life on the ocean and all I knew was that the voyage would be long, arduous, uncomfortable and possibly dangerous. As I said before, my uncle had paid for my passage, but only as a second-class passenger. I should not complain for the lot of the third-class passengers was to spend upwards of two months, depending on weather conditions, in exceedingly cramped accommodation where disease could break out at any time.

During the voyage, there were nineteen burials at sea, many of them children who had succumbed to illnesses brought on by a general lack of hygiene through having so many people thrown together, particularly in the steerage. Due to the cramped and overcrowded conditions in steerage, people could not really take baths and made do with a clean-up with a damp cloth under a blanket. Most people did not have the room to change their clothing and often wore the same garments or clothing for the entire voyage. Facilities for washing clothes were very restricted. The officers on board did their best, God knows they did; the areas below deck were thoroughly cleaned every few days by sailors and many of the women in steerage. Bedding which was usually made of straw, attracted fleas and cockroaches. People brought up their bedding in fine weather to shake it out and air it. However, in storms and bad weather, the bedding was often soaked through and this led to outbreaks of influenza and pneumonia. In the over-crowded conditions in steerage, epidemics were common. Most victims were babies and young children, who often died of complications and lack of medical care. Infected passengers often came on board, having passed undetected through pre-boarding medical checks. Tuberculosis was understandably one of the most dangerous diseases. For the burial, the body was sewn into a piece of canvas or placed in a rough coffin, often hastily knocked up by the ship's carpenter, and weighed down with pig iron or lead to help it sink. A plank had been placed on deck, one end over the ship's side, and upon this plank the sailors placed the body, covering it with an ensign. The sailors gently lifted the ensign and running out the plank and lifting up one end, the body dropped over the side into the water. It was one of the saddest sights I had ever encountered and Doctor Tawton took each death to heart in spite of doing all he possibly could to prolong their lives.

If I thought my time on board as his assistant would be plain sailing, excuse the pun, then I was rudely disabused of that notion in no time at all. By far the chief illness, temporary though it may have been and relatively harmless, was sea-sickness. As we suffered with it ourselves, we could readily sympathise with those similarly afflicted especially as sympathy was all we could offer in most cases. All that was still in the future as I prepared to take my place on the RMS Hellespont on a dull, overcast morning in Liverpool. She was a noble-looking ship, some four-hundred feet in length and I did have a momentary attack of panic at the thought of being confined on board this vessel for weeks and weeks, but I duly took my place and was even rather pleased with my cabin which was certainly comfortable, well-equipped if a little small. I sought out the medical quarters where Doctor Tawton was already laying out his equipment. We had met briefly at St Paul's during apposition[7].

He greeted me with 'Ah, Watson, my loblolly boy,' and then grinned at my mystified expression. The name itself comes from the serving of loblolly, a thick porridge,

---

[7] A public disputation by scholars; a formal examination by question and answer; still applied to the 'Speech day' at St Paul's School, London.

sometimes enhanced with chunks of meat or vegetables to sick or injured crewmembers to hasten their recovery. Loblolly, in turn, probably came from the fusion of lob, a Yorkshire word meaning to boil or bubble and lolly, an archaic English word for a stew or soup. The loblolly boy's duties included serving food to the sick, but also undertaking any medical tasks that the surgeon was too to perform. These included restraining patients during surgery, obtaining and cleaning surgical instruments, disposing of amputated limbs, and emptying and cleaning toilet utensils. The loblolly boy also often managed stocks of herbs, medicines and medical supplies.

As valuable as it may have proved to be for my medical education I managed to complete the voyage without restraining patients or disposing of amputated limbs. Besides, Tawton had his own official assistant, a Mr. Ransom, known as the sick berth attendant. Even though the term was already dated, I was known as the 'loblolly boy' for the rest of my time on board.[8] As I had in effect volunteered my services I was under no obligation to report to the medical quarters every day, but ever the conscientious young man, I presented myself to Tawton most days and even then I was not required for more than a few hours at a time. It was a comfortable enough voyage, but only as long as it took for the first storm to arrive. The waves grew so large that the vessel was dwarfed, riding up and down the mighty swelling sea like a child's toy. Inside the ship there was no staying still unless the person was anchored in place, for the floor was whatever surface gravity flung the sailors and passengers upon. In that

---

[8]The name comes from the serving of loblolly—a thick porridge, sometimes enhanced with chunks of meat or vegetables—to sick or injured crewmembers to hasten their recovery.

state they'd have prayed to Poseidon[9] himself if they thought it would do any good.

There was no mercy in that howling wind, no grace in the waves, only wrath and tempest. The cacophony of sound was overwhelming, not just of nature, but of furniture freed by the storm to roll around and crash into anything that stood in its way. A few hours later, this expression of nature at its wildest was just a memory. The sunshine bathed a becalmed ocean, shone off the rippling water, its golden light warped in the twisted, but gentle waves. No description can truly capture its mysterious majesty, yet only a few words can express its beauty. Perhaps only then I appreciated and respected the ocean we steamed across. As violent as that first storm was, it bore no comparison to those that came later especially as we neared the Cape of Good Hope[10].

The intensity of the tempests was terrifying even to experienced sailors who nevertheless kept to their routines admirably. My recourse was often just to shut myself up in my cabin, anchor myself down on my bunk and wait for the winds to abate. There were few young men on board among the passengers and even fewer young women. A second-class passenger is somehow neither fish nor fowl, feeling unable to socialise with those above or below. I made nodding acquaintances with various people when perambulating the deck in between medical duties and sitting out the frequent storms.

One young woman in particular intrigued me, a red-haired beauty whose hair remained vibrant day after day. Even keeping my hair clean presented a challenge to me

---

[9] The ancient Greek god of the sea, with the power to cause earthquakes, identified by the Romans with Neptune.

[10] A rocky headland on the Atlantic coast of the Cape Peninsula, South Africa

faced as it was with the daily assault from the wind, the sun when it chose to shine and sea salt which penetrated everything. My hair remained defiantly flat and lacklustre and must have been unappealing to any prospective admirer.

Being unexperienced as a suitor it took many days before I could pluck up the courage attempt a conversation with her aside from the mumbled greetings we already exchanged as we passed each other on the deck, at least when the days were sufficiently calm to enable such perambulations to take place. This inexperience of mine you will readily understand when I tell you that I spent hours in front of my mirror rehearsing my opening gambits of which there were many, all of them to remain unused for she literally fell at my feet one day when she tripped over a carelessly placed coil of rope. Thus, my opening gambits were reduced at once to an examination of her ankle and soothing comments and questions as to where it hurt!

Her name was Adeline Potter and she was travelling to Australia to be re-united with her father who had gone out to the goldfields of the country to seek his fortune as so many had before him. He was one of the fortunate ones and had made a fortune, albeit a small one as Adeline explained to me. With his gains, he bought a plot of land in a settlement named Moe[11], some eighty miles east of Melbourne. On this land, he had built a hotel which Adeline was going to assist in the running of. Her father, Andrew Potter, was of the belief that Moe was going to turn very quickly from a small settlement to a city in no time at all and he was determined to be in at the start of this growth.

Adeline's mother had parted from Andrew when Adeline was but six years old which is when Andrew decided to sail to the other side of the world. There had been sporadic

---

[11] A very small settlement then. Its name means 'swamp land'.

communication between daughter and father while he had been working the goldfields in search of the find he was always confident would come along. Once he had come into money he implored Adeline to come out to join him. She had steadfastly refused, her loyalties clearly resided with her mother.

However, her mother had recently died from consumption and with no kith or kin in England, she had made the decision to throw in her lot with her father and build a new life and rebuild her relationship with him. We had in common, therefore, the sense of starting a new life on a faraway continent although at that time I had not the notion of my domicile being permanent as hers would likely prove to be. We came to know each other very well as the voyage progressed and our daily walks were moments of great joy for me. I, had of course had to keep my mind focused on my duties in the sick bay, but we spent as much time together as was humanly possible. I do not as a rule agree with the modern trend, deplorable in my view, that memoirs have to include descriptions of intimacy that are better left unsaid, so I will not venture into the details of our growing romance.

Up until that point dear Lily was the only girl I had kissed and I was therefore quite a bashful suitor, but earnest, oh most definitely earnest. We made promises to each other that I hoped against hope would be binding, so smitten was I. There is a disturbing modern trend for people in the public eye to pen 'warts and all' memoirs. It is not a trend I am in favour of as I have just mentioned therefore you will look in vain for the level of intimacy I enjoyed with Adeline, suffice to say we considered ourselves betrothed even if it was only the two of us who were aware of it. Our time together was nearly at and end for as I went up on top the deck one morning I could see Williamstown, its buildings shimmering in the sun which had burst through the clouds as if in a greeting from the New World to us weary travellers. And there was no doubt, we were all very weary indeed.

From our vantage point on the deck Adeline spotted her father who was busily scanning the expectant faces nearby without recognising his daughter until she waved at him. His smile at that point was in direct contrast to how I was feeling. After weeks of Adeline's most delightful company, I was now not sure of when I would see her again, nor how her father would react to his daughter's admirer.

Before I took my leave of the ship and stepped ashore on to Australian soil, I had first to take my leave of Henry Tawton and Mr. Ransom. I had learned a great deal from both men during the voyage and their kindness and patience with me was a lesson in how to treat people that I have never forgotten and it was something I always tried to apply in my own career. Adeline's father was naturally inquisitive about the youth who accompanied his daughter down onto the quay. I recounted the incident of Adeline's ankle injury, possibly overplaying my medical role! I don't know how far I went in impressing the man, but he offered to buy me a breakfast as he explained that the coach to Moe was not leaving for two hours. I had no idea about the times of the train I needed other than it would involve a circuitous journey on two trains, first to Geelong than a second from there to Ballarat itself. Uppermost in my thoughts was that I would be over one hundred and fifty miles from Adeline. I very nearly reconsidered my agenda and instead go to Moe, but arrangements had been made and one hundred and fifty miles was hardly an insurmountable distance or barrier to romance.

I remember that morning of arrival in Melbourne so clearly, I can almost feel the warmth of the sun. Andrew Potter led us through to the streets to a small establishment on Spencer Street which sold sixpenny breakfasts. It was obviously very popular as obtaining a table was extremely difficult, but eventually we found ourselves seated in a far corner. The scene is etched on my mind in spite of the passage of time and my failing faculties. 'Breakfast, sir?' said the Irish waitress, who had expertly negotiated the crowded tables. 'Chops, steaks, sausages, fried fish, dry hash.' 'Stop,' I cried, aghast at this list of luxuries, 'I will have a cup of tea and some bread and butter.' 'What else, sir? There's nice steak this morning.' 'How much is a steak?' I asked, bent on economy for the sake of Andrew Potter's purse in spite of the man smiling broadly at me. 'Sixpence, sir.' 'And the tea, and bread and butter?' 'All sixpence.' That I could obtain soup, meat, and pastry for the ridiculously small sum of sixpence was a revelation of inestimable value and incidentally it was not the last time that I was to feel like a fish out of water in that continent.

Adeline's father talked of his plans for his hotel in Moe, The Digger's Rest. He was confident that the rapid expansion that had already been seen, due in no small part to the gold rush, would be replicated in Moe and he was determined to be in on it and provide a future for Adeline. I felt a pang of distress for it was me who should be providing a future for her, for us. True, I had little to offer her in terms of security or prosperity, but naively I thought love would conquer all. It has often been my undoing.

After the last of the dishes had been cleared away I knew the time of farewell was on us. It was all very proper and formal, we shook hands while reiterating as best we could those promises we intended to keep to each other. Andrew Potter shook my hand and they walked away to catch the coach. At the end of the street before they turned the corner, Adeline turned and smiled, knowing I would still be watching. I was not to know it would be my last ever sight of her.

Cylinder 4

The train to Geelong[12] was overcrowded, dangerously so in my opinion, but everyone on board took it in their stride so I assumed this was commonplace for the journey. The second half of the journey from Geelong to Ballarat was less crowded, and I was able to relax at last. The landscape between the two towns was quite unlike anything I had ever seen. One moment, desert, the next, dense woodland. It was an ever-changing kaleidoscope of colour. I marvelled at the ingenuity of the engineers who had forged their way through this country, the tracks remaining straight and true even though the undulations of the land and natural barriers would have created numerous difficulties.

My enthusiasm for this temporary new life of mine had been dimmed since meeting Adeline and the excitement I had once felt for coming to Ballarat was considerably subdued.

---

[12] 75km from Melbourne. During the gold rush Geelong experienced a brief boom as the main port to the rich goldfields of the Ballarat district.

Back in England, I had made contact with a doctor in the city who had agreed to having my occasional help and assistance in return for food and lodging. Doctor Joseph Josephs, a victim of his parents' humour in his Christian name maybe, was a prominent member of the community of the newly proclaimed city. His brother, Henry was mayor of the borough at that time. I suspected my help would prove to be more than occasional and so it proved to be. Ballarat had the look of a much older city although it had not been in existence for all that long, something it shared in common with many other Australian towns and cities. It was not quite the Ballarat I had imagined.

Gold mining was slowing down considerably as was lead mining, and the city appeared to be in a depression. The changes in mining had resulted in a migration that had halted the population growth which had enjoyed a rapidity of growth just as at Melbourne. Nevertheless, there were many plans to rejuvenate the city and to enhance daily life for its residents. I was there for what I supposed would be an adventure, but on arrival in Ballarat, I was full of doubts as to what exactly I was doing. Why had I travelled the other side of the world on little more than a whim? A whim based on a book I had read as a child.

However, I could scarcely turn back and I duly made my way, bags in hand to the home and surgery of Doctor Josephs which was situated on…it was on…ah Sturt Street, that was it. A large house, which sat in the middle of a business district. The ground floor was where the surgery and waiting-room were situated, along with a kitchen which backed on to a small yard. The second floor was given over to four bedrooms and a large reception room. Joseph Josephs was a rather stern-looking man, with hair that looked as though it had a permanent gale blowing through it, so unruly was it. If his name offered me a degree of amusement, imagine my surprise upon being introduced to his wife, Josephine. I was less practiced at keeping a straight face in those days, but somehow, I managed it.

My room was comfortable enough with ample storage space, a single iron-framed bed and a desk. I had a notion at the time to keep a journal detailing my adventures, should there be any, during my time in Australia. I never did find the time to undertake such a task which is a great shame as a notebook of the kind would come in very handy right now. One of Joseph's first actions was to thrust a book into my hand, written, as I recall, by a local journalist, which was a richly detailed history of Ballarat. That is another book which would come in handy right now. I protested that I was quite well up in the history of the area, but my protestations were swept aside and I acquiesced. 'Read it cover to cover, mind' he admonished. I thought for a brief moment that he was about to tell me how he would question me on it daily.

The city was remarkable for what I saw then was a thriving, although less so of late, city with forty thousand inhabitants living where twenty years ago there was not even one house, but enormous amounts of activity would have been seen with gold fields being worked, the mines in full flow and outside of that there would have been only the solitude of the wild primeval forest, now tamed by man. It was incredible to think that the long lines of stately buildings, the elegant shops and the huge factories could have sprung up in such a short space of time.

Over the course of my first few days in Ballarat, I covered the whole area on foot, traversing the old workings on the gold fields. In Leigh valley, I observed the sandstone foundations of a station which had remained unbuilt. Those unfinished walls were in a paddock overlooking a little carse of some four or five acres by the creek side, close to the junction of the Woolshed Creek, with the main stream in the valley.

On the other side of the larger stream rise basaltic mounds, marked with the pits and banks of the earlier miners. Like the trenches of an old battlefield, these works of the digging armies of the past were now grass-grown and spotted with wild flowers. All around, the open lands of twenty years ago had been turned into streets and fields and gardens.

Whenever I think of Ballarat that is the image I see. Perhaps it was the same for the old diggers of two decades before. For those who stayed, how many enjoyed this expansion of the city from such humble beginnings? Did they see it as magical? Did they see their own lives as diggers magical? It certainly seemed that way to be in the stories of the gold rush I had read, but reality sings a different song. I pictured an old digger now as he walked about those spacious gas-lit streets, where he no longer has need of the candle in the broken bottle as a lantern after dark, but where every thoroughfare is adorned with crowding edifices and is glittering with the blaze of a more artificial life and the results of accumulated wealth. As he looks, perhaps there come moments when all the scene dissolves into its original elements. Through all the rattle of street strife, over all the display of churches, towers, halls and noisy warehouses, his eyes see something and his ears hear something invisible and inaudible to others. Over all the array of aggregated civic opulence and beauty and its dark shadows of want and haggard strife for bread, there steal to him the silence of the beginning, a few white tents among the forest trees that are no more; the half-dozen columns of curling smoke from the camp fires; the round, oval and square pits of the shallow-ground digger; the scanty patches of newly turned up golden soil. The fresh breeze that came over the old silent odorous bush and its reaches of grass-land, breathes upon him again instead of the noisome exhalations from the gutters and sewers and by-ways of the thickly peopled city. In another moment that scene, too, glides past and reality and the present impose itself.

The old diggers I spoke to were certainly more prone to looking back than looking forward and for such tough, uncompromising men they all had a touch of wistfulness that clung to them. The site of the Eureka stockade action which so thrilled me as a boy was disappointing. There was nothing left of the buildings and nothing there that recorded the event. It seemed conveniently forgotten if not by the people, then certainly the authorities who apparently had no wish to commemorate the violence of that event.

Once the excitement of my early forays into the city had paled, I settled down into a routine; assisting Doctor Josephs when required which was often enough and nothing like the comparatively light tasks I had been entrusted with on the ship. I can honestly say I worked extremely hard for my board and lodgings. To me, the atmosphere of the city, notwithstanding the industry, was quite healthy. The endless queues of patients streaming to our door testified of something else. It wasn't a malady that could in most cases be whittled down to a handful of common ailments.

There was a malady of the mind at work. The obsession the diggers had shown when they were hunting for gold now turned into other obsessions; food, drink, smoking and diseases arising from the access the men had to easy women. I tried my level best to get to the root of these problems by sitting the men down, eighty percent of all our patients were men, and talking to them. Not just talking of course, but listening. Doctor Josephs was none too pleased with these sessions of mine; he was only too glad to see the back of most of them. Not that I am casting aspersions on his medical abilities. I wasn't then and I am not now. We were just different in our approach.

Once a week or sometimes twice a week I wrote a letter to Adeline. Looking back to my youth, I can acknowledge now that they were unnecessarily florid and romantic, but there was no doubt in my mind that I was in love and I had no reason to suppose that Adeline did not reciprocate my feelings. The replies were fairly swift in coming and I would carry her letters with me everywhere and read them so often that they were in danger of falling apart. The news was that the hotel was doing well and she had settled in very well. She expressed the wish that we would meet before too long.

Later letters took longer to arrive and left me frustrated and worried out of my mind. The missives that did arrive were now somehow impersonal and concentrated on events at the hotel and township rather than her feelings, hopes and dreams. There was often a mention of a Veerhoeven, A Dutchman whom her father had taken on to oversee the completion of the hotel. I should have seen it coming of course. It is no wonder they say love is blind. Three months later, Adeline's father sent me a letter simply stating that Adeline had married Dirk Veerhoeven a few days before.

The news stopped me dead in my tracks. It was as though my whole future had become a thing of nonsense that I wanted no part of. The Josephs' were very patient with this madman they had taken into their house who had suddenly become incapable of even the simplest of duties. They say there's no fool like an old fool, at my age I am entitled to say it, but I think it is equally so that there is no fool like a young fool. Gradually, this madness, and I don't use the word lightly, passed, and life went back to a form of normality.

I even began to enjoy life in Ballarat anew for the truth was that this city that had sprung out of nowhere was filled with such vibrancy and growth that it was impossible not to be caught up in it. There was no Rugby club to immerse myself in, but cricket was played to a fairly high standard and I was invited to join the ranks, not that I was especially a cricketer of note, but I gave it my all and managed to pick up a fair few runs if rather less by way of wickets! I remember well the fierce rivalry between Ballarat and Geelong in spite of the first match between the sides having taken place only a few years before. The Eastern oval was, in those days at least, a fairly ramshackle place with shady fish ponds surrounded by trees. The grandstand was a large wooden building with a skittle alley made of interlaced sticks with a thatched roof. Behind this building there was a bowling green.

On rainy days, of which there were plenty, we would fill our time playing skittles...for money. I was often out of pocket particularly as the losers were expected to stand a round of beers at the Lewis Pavilion Hotel which had the distinction of being the only fully licensed hotel on a sports ground in the state of Victoria.

There was a rumour, unconfirmed like all good rumours should be, that WG Grace[13] would be touring Australia in the winter of 1873/1874 and there was further talk that he would be bringing his troops to Ballarat. It had been my plan to be back in England by then to pick up the reins of my education, but the thought of being involved in a splendid sporting occasion began to sway me towards thoughts of staying longer. I gave in to those thoughts of course and duly advised the University of London that I would be taking up their offer a few months later than planned.

When time allowed, I would hire a horse and ride out into the countryside. It was a striking landscape, its beauty rugged, its splendours haphazard. There was a myriad of insects and spiders that seemed to be hell-bent on destroying

---

[13] England's foremost cricketer of 'The Golden Age'.

any of humankind they came across, many filled with enough poison to fell a horse let alone a man. I remember guiding my horse through a lightly wooded area as the sun dropped in the sky and shot rays between the trees. Glistening in between two trees was the largest web I had ever seen. And sitting motionless in it was the largest spider I had ever encountered. I am not one to affix human attributes to any member of the animal kingdom, but believe me, that spider was mean. Angry and mean. I had no real idea what it could do to me, but I was not about to stay and find out. I turned the horse around and rode fast for Ballarat. It was hardly a comforting thought that if the insects and spiders did not get you, then the snakes would! The sight of my first kangaroo was quite a moment I can tell you, but very quickly subsequent sightings became commonplace. Familiarity etc.

The talk of WG Grace's impending visit became bit by bit more than hearsay and arrangements were under way to receive our renowned visitors. The match was set to be played in the first week of January and it was decided that it would be a match which pitched twenty-two men of Ballarat against the eleven of Grace's team as there was an understandable gulf in class between the two sides. It was to be termed Ballarat against All England. Even with such a numerical advantage, Ballarat would not be expected to win although they certainly would expect to put up a good show. I entertained no hopes of playing in the match; there were other stalwarts of the cricket club who deserved their chance to play against such illustrious opposition. I was, after all, to all intents and purposes a visitor to the city.

However, a fortuitous chain of circumstances conspired to give me the opportunity of walking out onto the Eastern oval[14] to face Doctor Grace. For one, the date of the match coincided with the annual Caledonian gathering which laid claim to being the largest and grandest fete in the area. Some of those who could reasonably be expected to be part of the twenty-two found their loyalties torn and three or four had no choice but to withdraw from selection. Add to that, a dog bite, a calamity involving a runaway horse and an overturned carriage and suddenly I found myself in the twenty-two and with a, perhaps, ill-deserved nod to the few runs I had garnered in previous matches I was to enter the fray at number four in the batting line-up.

When Grace and his team rolled into the city they were greeted by the mayor who treated them to a fine luncheon. In the afternoon Grace inspected the pitch which he declared to be a fine piece of turf. He expressed some surprise at the short boundaries which he thought would play into the tourist's hands. He was proved right for over the course of the first two days' play, they racked up 470 runs with Grace and his brother, George, commonly known as Fred, making centuries. We had of course twenty-two fielders which you think would be number enough to keep the score down, but we struggled in the field with many hits simply going over our heads. I must also add in defence of our fielding that it was a very hot day and standing in the field under a broiling sun while batsmen played merry was no easy thing.

In spite of the Caledonian gathering, the attendance was very good indeed; six to seven thousand was the estimate. That the batting of the tourists was the principal attraction was not in doubt for on the third day when it was our turn at the wicket we found the crowd had fallen away considerably. We made a good match of it with the Figgis brothers making

---

[14] The Eastern Oval was host to one of the Test matches in the infamous 'Bodyline' series between Australia and England 1932/33.

eighty odd runs between them. I was lucky enough to make thirty-three runs before being out legged before wicket to WG Grace himself. No shame in that I told myself. At the close of the third and final day the score for Ballarat stood at 276 and the match was declared a draw. The local newspaper reported that I had made my runs in a cricket-like manner which seemed to be another way of saying that my batting was not the most exciting on view! When we came off the field we found champagne bottles lined up on a table in the luncheon room. We needed no second invitation to partake. Once the match and the celebrations were over, my thoughts were of my return to England which could be put off no longer.

Cylinder 5

I certainly had mixed feelings the day of my departure from Ballarat. From being a complete stranger, I had in my way become part of that community. I had been accepted as so many others had been accepted there before me. But now it was time to leave. I was leaving behind friends, but confident that the new chapter of my life would result in friendships that would hopefully prove to be just as strong.

The voyage home was long and just as arduous as the outward journey with no diversions to take up my time, nor indeed any worthwhile occupation. I kept myself to myself mostly and resolved that if any damsels in distress were to twist or sprain ankles in my vicinity then I would do my level best to ignore them. I had kept my uncle informed of my plans not that I was expecting any kind of welcoming committee when I embarked at Liverpool. I would have liked to head north to Hexham, but a lack of funds meant that the journey to London would have to be immediate.

I felt as though my education was complete with my doctoring, yes, I think it can be called that, on board the

Hellespont and my work in Ballarat, but in reality, I had four years of hard work approaching before being let loose in the world...somehow, somewhere. In the field of medicine things were changing very quickly. Sophia Jex-Blake[15] was leading the way for women to be allowed to take their degrees in medicine, something that just did not happen in those times. She argued that natural instinct leads women to concern themselves with the care of the sick. However, with education of girls being restricted to domestic crafts, women generally could not qualify to compete with men as medical practitioners. However, she argued that there was no objective proof of women's intellectual inferiority to men. She said that the matter could easily be tested by granting women 'a fair field and no favour' -- teaching them as men were taught and subjecting them to exactly the same examinations.

This seemed perfectly sound and logical to me and I wholeheartedly agreed with her sentiments. It was only 1870 when the University of Edinburgh admitted women in spite of fervent opposition. But and there is always a but. As the women began to demonstrate that they could compete on equal terms with the male students, hostility towards them began to grow. They received obscene letters, were followed home, had fireworks attached to their front door, mud thrown at them. This culminated in the Surgeons' Hall[16] riot on the 18th November 1870 when the women arrived to sit an anatomy exam at Surgeons' Hall and an angry mob of over

---

[15]Sophia Louisa Jex-Blake was an English physician, teacher and feminist. She led the campaign to secure women access to a University education.

[16]Surgeons' Hall in Edinburgh, Scotland, is the headquarters of the Royal College of Surgeons of Edinburgh. It houses the Surgeons' Hall Museum, and the library and archive of the RCSED.

two hundred were gathered outside throwing mud, rubbish and insults at the women.

The events made national headlines and won the women many new supporters. However, influential members of the medical faculty eventually persuaded the university to refuse graduation to the women and the campaign in Edinburgh failed in 1873. Many of the women went to European universities that were already allowing women to graduate and completed their studies there.

It was as I arrived in London that Doctor Jex-Blake was setting up the London School of Medicine for Women. They were exciting times. Life in Forest Hill, however, was just the same. My uncle was still holding the reins of his business empire and Mrs Chinneck was still running around after him. I moved back into my old room, feeling like a schoolboy again. I suppose that's what I was…an overgrown schoolboy with still so much to learn. The University of London would see me through to my goals, most of which to be honest were not exactly clear to me.

Did I want to have my own medical practice? Did I want to become a surgeon? To open a medical practice, I would need to be a member of The Royal College of Surgeons and a licence from the Royal College of Physicians. My life quickly became a round of learning in the greatest detail whole swathes of information on chemistry, physics, botany, anatomy and physiology. My aptitude for learning was as strong as it had ever been and in spite of feeling that life was one weary trudge through textbooks, I took in what I needed and probably an awful lot more I didn't. Most of my training took place at Barts [17] within the confines of St. Bartholomew's Hospital Medical College.

---

[17] Barts is the oldest hospital in Britain still providing medical services which occupies the site it was originally built on, and has an

The journey there replicated the journey I had made to St Paul's. I alighted at the same station and walked to Smithfield. The days were shorter than they were at school for which I was grateful. Some days were entirely spent in watching operations being performed whilst the surgeon in charge kept us regaled with a commentary of what he was doing and why. One unfortunate student standing by me one day, during a particularly intricate and quite bloody surgical procedure, fainted clean away. I was made of sterner stuff which I was to find out a few years later after the battle of Maiwand.

But once more, I digress. My attention wanders often, not just speaking into this cylinder, but throughout my life. The memories of my youth I am relating contrast so wildly with what my life has become, it's difficult to carry on. That early vitality has all but gone. I know, it's life. But it doesn't make it any easier. I'll take a short break to compose myself.

I was able to reacquaint myself with St Paul's through being invited to play rugby for the old boys' team, the Paulinians. I was also fortunate enough to renew my association with the Blackheath club. Sport was the perfect antidote for the hours of tedium I often had to endure in my studies. Even allowing for that tedium I worked hard to ensure my grades would be of a standard high enough to earn my diploma without too much by way of re-visiting of topics. It was certainly a long four years. But I was fortunate enough to make some good friends during my time there.

The first of these was Godfrey Jacobs, who was a very attentive and capable student, but also a very fine sportsman.

---

important current role as well as a long history and architecturally important buildings.

I cajoled him into trying out for Blackheath[18] which he did with great success, becoming an influential member of the side, whose play-making was a thing of beauty. We shared many glorious moments in some of Blackheath's famous victories.

After we had both completed our university courses we ended up at opposite ends of the country and although we corresponded fitfully, we did not meet again for just over twenty years later when he became mixed up in a baffling crime in Lyme Regis[19] where he had settled some years before. It was an adventure for myself and Holmes, the like of which we had never known before.

But once more, I get ahead of myself, that is a tale that I will come to later. It was at Barts that I first met Arthur Thurston who would remain a friend for many years. Poor old Thurston, he used to rag us on our sporting abilities while laying claim to some of his own. His only pastime, however, was billiards which we pointed out was a game not a sport. Mind you, he was very skilled as I found out many a time over the years and in the process losing a few shillings to him. Well, maybe it was pounds. I was never one to turn down a wager, even when I could least afford it.

In the early part of 1874 the scorecard from the Ballarat match against Grace's team was published in the press here. I was immensely proud of my innings and pointed out to

---

[18]The institution was founded as "Blackheath Football Club" in 1858 by old boys of Blackheath Proprietary School who played a "carrying" game of football made popular by Rugby School. When the old boys played against the current pupils, supporters would shout for either "Club" or "School" accordingly.

[19]Lyme Regis is a coastal town in West Dorset, England, situated 25 miles west of Dorchester and 25 miles east of Exeter. The town lies in Lyme Bay, on the English Channel coast at the Dorset–Devon border. It is nicknamed "The Pearl of Dorset.

everyone I knew, my feats as printed there, 'Look, that was me.' Much to my chagrin, no one believed me. I tried in vain to claim my moment of fame, but to no avail. It must have been another Watson they said. It was just a coincidence you were in Ballarat at same time they said.

In truth, I scarcely played cricket after that apart from a few club matches and although I watched WG Grace on many occasions I never had the chance to speak to the man again, not that we were great conversationalists in Australia. Lest you think my life completely revolved around sport at this time, let me assure you I was just as diligent in my studies. I was very much part of a man's world and I enjoyed the comradeship which made me think of perhaps joining the army as a surgeon. It would continue the comradeship I had come to value plus it would enable me to travel once more to far flung outposts of the Empire. It was not a decision that had to be made immediately, however. I was, at that time, quite guarded with my heart.

My experience with Adeline had left me emotionally bruised and battered and I was in no hurry to dive back into the world of romance. Yet, I did step out with a young lady or two during my university days in spite of being entrenched in that man's world I described. They were not serious affiliations in any sense of the word, but pleasant enough all the same and no promises were made or sought on either side.

Caught up as I was in my own life I failed to notice the cracks that were beginning to appear in my uncle's life. The regimens of the household life became less structured. The order to his life which he swore by was becoming random even chaotic. Mrs Chinneck was at her wits end and I was little help. My uncle was not a man that could be approached easily on any topic and truth be told, I had no great desire to approach him. We were not close and whilst I was certainly grateful for all he had done for me, I did not feel any special kinship with him. His detached, aloof manner did not encourage such bonds to form. He, himself, expressed no inclination to speak of what was troubling him.

I asked Mrs Chinneck what she knew of this change in my uncle's behaviour. She mentioned the words 'financial irregularities', and 'debts and debtors', whispered them as though the very walls had ears. I surmised that walls and doors had given up this information to her. She could eavesdrop so well and with such ease. Holmes would have been proud of her.

This uncertain state of affairs continued for several more weeks until one day, after a weekend away in Southsea, I came home to an empty house. There were three envelopes propped up on the mantelpiece for me. Two contained notes for me from my uncle and Mrs Chinneck respectively and the other contained a bundle of banknotes with a scribbled note to invest wisely. My uncle and Mrs Chinneck had set sail for India over the course of that weekend having emptied his bank accounts, presumably to leave nothing left in the kitty for debtors. The amount of money left for me, if I kept away from the racetracks, would comfortably see out my final two years at university assuming I could find digs at a reasonable rate. I never did get to the bottom of my uncle's malpractice if indeed it were malpractice.

By far the most surprising thing about the whole affair was the news that was reinforced in both letters; namely, that my uncle and Mrs Chinneck were to be married! I had no means of congratulating them on this unexpected news for I had no address for them and once I had left the house at Forest Hill they would not have one for me either although a note to Barts would find me if they so wished. They didn't.

The house had already been sold as I was to find out the following morning when the house agents arrived with the new tenants. I collected as many as my belongings as I could and skulked away. I bunked down a couple of nights at Thurston's family home in Fulham and once I had deposited my windfall in the bank I set about finding somewhere to live. I was fortunate enough to find two rooms in a narrow lane off Fleet Street which was close enough to Barts to enable me to luxuriate in an extra hour in bed each morning. Even allowing for that luxury, I was still managed to be late on occasion.

My tardiness was already an issue. In later years, I would get it down to a fine art. I was now looked on as a man of means by my fellow students and to keep that up I started to spend way above those perceived means. Somewhere along the line, probably when I had lost a hefty wager I came to my senses and became a tad more frugal. During my third year I finally made that decision which had been brewing for some time; I decided to join the army as a surgeon, if they wanted me of course.

It may surprise some of you that know me through my accounts of Holmes's adventures that, I, the upstanding John H Watson has in fact a criminal record. I suppose I can look back on it now and laugh, but at the time I was mortified. The incident took place after a match between Blackheath and our bitter rivals, Richmond[20]. It is no idle boast to say that it was my finest match, everything I did that day came off; my kicking and handling of the ball was as precise as it was ever

---

[20]Formed in 1861, it is one of the oldest football clubs in the world and holds a significant place in the history of Rugby Football, playing in the first ever match under the rules of the Football Association on 19 December 1863, against the Barnes Club, even though it was not a member of the RFA. In 1878 it hosted the first ever floodlit match and in 1909 played in the inaugural match at Twickenham Stadium, the home of English Rugby.

to be. Jacobs, too, was magnificent that day. When the final whistle blew, we were both chaired off the pitch by our grateful teammates.

That kind of adulation, temporary though it may have been, can go to a man's head. It certainly did to ours. Having arrived back in the city in the middle of the evening, we met up with some fellow students who were only too willing to assist in our celebrations. These celebrations demanded that a fairly large amount of alcohol be consumed. I was not a great drinker then, even less so now and it was not long before I began to lose control over events. I have it on the best authority that the police constable had done nothing to enrage me so it was a surprise to my companions when I charged into him and ran off with his helmet for an imagined try-line. By the time I had touched the helmet down in High Holborn [21] the shrill sound of his police whistle had summoned the aid of two burly constables who tackled me to the ground in no uncertain manner.

The ensuing night in the police cells was certainly chastening. Even more so was my appearance in the police-court in the morning. After being lectured by the magistrate for an unfeasibly long time I was fined ten shillings and bound over to keep the peace for a year. I was then free to leave the court and slink away to my rooms to nurse my headache. Of course, I endured some ribbing when my hangover eased enough for me to attend the medical school the following day. And yet there was yet another lecture on morals by one of the professors who no doubt had seen this kind of thing many times, but he was no less severe on me because of that fact. It was to be my last brush with the law.

---

[21] A street in the Holborn area of central London.

Cylinder 6

I made some notes yesterday evening to help me with this session, but have managed to misplace them. I am constantly losing things these days. I have found that revisiting my past has unaccountably aided my memory so perhaps I will be able to get by without them. The Royal Victoria Military Hospital at Netley was my next port of call after obtaining my degree of Doctor of Medicine.

The prescribed course for military surgeons was of six months duration, and studies were in military surgery, military medicine, hygiene and pathology. The hospital had been opened in 1863 thanks primarily to the concerted efforts of Florence Nightingale[22] who had witnessed horrors during the Crimean War[23]that made her determined to pioneer better

[22] Florence Nightingale, OM, RRC, DStJ was an English social reformer and statistician, and the founder of modern nursing.

[23]The Crimean War was a military conflict fought from October 1853 to February 1856 in which the Russian Empire lost to an alliance of the Ottoman Empire, France, Britain and Sardinia.

medical treatment for wounded soldiers. That the hospital was to open without adhering to her plans was not her fault of course. I suppose some would say it was better than nothing which it certainly was.

My course began in April of 1879 and at that point my funds were dwindling somewhat. At least my board and lodging at the hospital would be paid for and after that, the army would be my only source of income. The hospital was in a pleasant enough location, set in a large area of land bordered by the River Itchen and River Hamble just to the east of Southampton. It was certainly imposing; the main building was reckoned to be the longest in the world at that time. The building was enormous, grand, and visually attractive, but was neither convenient nor practical. Corridors were on the sea-facing front of the building, leaving the wards facing the inner courtyard with little light and air. Ventilation in general was poor, with unpleasant smells lingering around the vast building.

I cannot say in all honesty that I enjoyed my time there, but it was a means to an end and besides it was only six months that I had to endure there. Early patients arriving from campaigns taking place all over the world during the expansion of the British Empire had an uncomfortable journey to the hospital, either having to be transferred to a shallow-draft boat if landing at the pier or transported from Netley station to the hospital if arriving by rail. More often than not, the men were more disheartened by their arrival at the hospital, but even for them of course, it was a means to an end. It was quite a sight in spite of its flaws. The hospital was, after all, a town in itself, a two hundred-acre metropolis with its own gasworks, reservoir, school, stables, bakery and prison. There was a grand officers' mess, complete with ballroom, and modest married quarters for other ranks. There was even a salty swimming pool, fed by a windmill pumping water from the sea. It was known to everyone as Spike Island, a local name for that area.

Now, what a good title for a story; Sherlock Holmes and the Mystery of Spike Island. But I digress again. The hours were long and arduous. Rest, proper rest that is, was never easy to come by and the discipline was harsh. After all, for us students it was all about preparing us for life in the army where discipline may be a matter of life and death. I made no real friends there and I missed the ones I had; Thurston remained in London, working in Camberwell and Jacobs had found employment as a general practitioner in Manchester from where he would send me amusing letters of his life in the industrial north.

I did take an interest in one of the nurses, a Miss Emily…damn…what was her surname? Fortescue? Fothergill? Ah, I have it…it was Fotheringay. She was a very dainty girl and I was not the only one to take an interest. I had a rival. Hah! I have always had rivals it seems to me. We took occasional walks along the banks of the Hamble when our periods of free time coincided. When they didn't marry up, then she took similar walks with Robert…er…well, Robert something anyway. We were actually pals as well as rivals, but blessed if I can remember his name. It is of no import for neither of us got the girl and none of us ever met again. She fell for a doctor who possessed more in way of charm than Robert or me between us. That was quite a blow to my masculinity for I considered my charm was one of my more appealing qualities to the opposite sex, something Sherlock Holmes would allude to on more than one occasion.

Truth be told, at that stage of my life I had not formed a lasting relationship; oh, I may have considered myself to be in love on a few occasions, but even that was open to doubt. My immediate future would be tied up to the fortunes or otherwise of the army which promised not to be conducive to romance. My experience at Netley did prove that discipline could be instilled in me which was obviously a major part of army life.

At this stage, I had no inkling where I would be posted or even with which regiment. I had not given the matter too much thought; it wasn't as if I were going to have any choice in the matter. It was almost my last week at Netley when I received my orders, namely that I would be attached to the 5th Northumberland Fusiliers[24], that grand old regiment as the assistant surgeon. It meant my first posting was to India, to Bombay in fact, where the regiment was stationed.

Once again, I prepared to leave my home shores for a distant land. I was intrigued as to whether I would come to any knowledge of my uncle and his new wife, not that there would be time for anything but pressing army activities of course, but the notion intrigued me. It was an uncertain time in the east. The consensus from all the political commentators of the day, judging by the newspaper accounts I read was that a war between Britain and Afghanistan was unavoidable. I was almost on the point of departure when the news came that Sher Ali Khan[25], the Emir of Afghanistan had turned away a British mission headed by Lord Lyttelton. This was enough to trigger war.

---

[24]The Northumberland Fusiliers traces its origin to 1674 as one of the Holland Regiments in the service of the Prince of Orange. In 1836 it was converted into a Fusilier Regiment, as the 5th (Northumberland Fusiliers) for having defeated a French Division of Grenadiers at Wilhemstahl (1762). From that date onwards, it bore a badge of a flaming grenade with St George at its centre.

[25]Sher Ali Khan was Amir of Afghanistan from 1863 to 1866 and from 1868 until his death in 1879. He was the third son of Dost Mohammed Khan, founder of the Barakzai Dynasty in Afghanistan.

Gilchrist, that was his name. Robert that is, my love rival. Just popped into my head. These days things are more likely to leave my head.

It was a fine and sunny Saturday morning when I packed my bags and took the train to Portsmouth where I would board a ship to India. How did I feel? Excited? Apprehensive? I knew I was now heading into a war with all the horrors that would entail. I am not ashamed to admit I was having grave doubts about this decision of mine to follow a military career. The notion of adventure had taken me this far, but now I was faced with the reality of what it would mean to serve in the army. I hoped my doctoring skills were up to the standards and I hoped my nerve would hold under the extreme conditions I was likely to find.

We steamed out of Portsmouth on the *Tigris*. The conditions were basic even for the officers amongst us, but so much better than the poor souls who suffered on the journey out to Australia, so fresh in my memory. The crossing was smooth and uneventful. So much so that very little of it has remained in my memory. The events that followed were a different kettle of fish. And besides I made extensive notes after the events which follow that I have beside me now.

On disembarkation at Bombay I reported to the Army Medical Department who eventually managed to guide me through the forms, often in triplicate, that confirmed my appointment with my regiment. The only fly in the ointment was that the Northumberland Fusiliers were already well on their way to Afghanistan therefore with barely a moment to myself I was on my travels again.

Firstly, a steamer to Karachi which was undoubtedly the easy part of the journey, but even so lasted a few days. The onward journey from Karachi was initially by train. Oh, that train! So hot, so stuffy and so overcrowded. Illness was rife especially what may be termed politely as stomach bugs.

Once it was known I was a doctor I was deluged by poor souls who were desperate for some alleviation from their suffering. Ordinarily, I would have prescribed fresh water to be their only diet for a few days, but fresh water was a commodity in short supply.

However, I did what I could. On reaching the railhead we found a wagon train being hastily assembled from such supplies that had made it that far. Precious little by way of weaponry which was scarcely reassuring although the medical supplies were pleasingly comprehensive, even down to portable operating tables. God knows, I remember thinking, we would have need of them soon enough.

It was a long march for the majority of the men, who were not as great in number as I had anticipated. Some of the officers rode on horses or camels. Some were reduced to riding on mules. It was a landscape of extremes with weather to match. The long days were stiflingly hot yet when night fell the temperatures would drop quickly and reminded me forcibly of Northumberland winters.

Our destination was Kandahar and when we entered the city it had been over a month since leaving Bombay. Once again, I was foiled in my attempt join my regiment for they had moved on once more; this time to the northern territories where they formed part of the Peshawar Valley Field Force[26]. The adjutant in command of the garrison at Kandahar took it upon himself to attach me to the Royal Berkshires, the 66th. At least I was to be spared another journey for a while. I was not, however, spared any duties.

---

[26] The Peshawar Valley Field Force was a British field force of around 12,000 men, a mix of both British regiments and South Asian regiments, under the command of Sir Samuel J. Browne during the Second Anglo-Afghan War (1878-1880).

As the weeks went by in that dry, dusty city I had a huge list of patients to attend to. These were chiefly illnesses brought about by the food and drink available and the severe heat. The 66th was the only British regiment stationed in Kandahar at that time. The numbers of fighting men were bolstered by units of the Indian cavalry, infantry and artillery including the 3rd Scinde Horse and the Bombay cavalry. There was also a group of Afghan soldiers who gave their allegiance equally to Wali Shere Ali, who was set to assume control of the city when the British forces pulled out, and to our military leaders. Amongst the officers and indeed the men there was certainly a lack of confidence in these Afghan troops. The consensus was that a mutiny was in the cards and when push came to shove, they would be found fighting us as opposed to fighting with us.

In the meantime, we were in limbo, defending a city from non-existent attackers and unable to engage the enemy elsewhere. This state of affairs changed suddenly when we received intelligence that the army of Ayub Khan was intent on marching on and destroying Kandahar. The decision was made to mobilise the men and march out to intercept this Afghan force. Our fighting force was no more than 2,500 men under the command of Brigadier-General Burrows who was not exactly the most experienced of officers. The Wali of Kandahar urged Burrows to confront Ayub and his men at Girishk on the Helmond river; he feared that if Ayub Khan had the chance to march further it would only serve to strengthen his numbers.

As we marched onwards, the Afghan troops within our force, supposedly loyal to us, acted exactly how some of us had feared by deserting in droves. Our troops engaged and defeated the rebellious Afghans and captured some valuable weaponry. Burrows then fell back to a position at Kushk-i-Nakhud, halfway to Kandahar where he could intercept Ayub

Khan if he headed for either Ghazni or Kandahar. We remained there a week, although it seemed longer for all of us, during which time the captured guns were added to our force with additional gunners drawn from the British infantry.

Eventually this hiatus came to an end when it was learned Ayub's army was on the move and was making for the Maiwand pass which was just a few miles from us. We could have marched in an instant, I firmly believe that. We were ready and some would say eager for battle, my own internal conflict notwithstanding. My job was to save lives not take them, but I was a serving member of the British army and my duty was to assist in every way possible. Should that mean taking lives of the enemy then so be it. The men in the ranks had a simple view of the matter; them or us, kill or be killed.

The delay of a few hours meant as it turned out that we had no chance of reaching Maiwand before the enemy. It was apparent that the strength of Ayub's army was still a mystery. The officers in charge, I think anyway, had recklessly and dangerously underestimated the number of men we would be facing. As we approached Maiwand, Ayub's army could be seen marching across our front, in the swirling dust storms that swept the semi-desert area. Burrows still formed the view, flying in the face of reason and facts, that he could reach Maiwand before the Afghans and urged his troops forward. It was not to be.

We passed the village of Mundabad and found we had reached a substantial ravine, twenty-five feet deep, running along its front. Instead of taking up defensive positions along the ravine and in the village, Burrows ordered the men across the ravine into the open plain beyond. If he was given advice of a sounder nature, then he did not act on it. It was at this time that the extent of the force opposing us could be gauged.

Of course, we could not actively count them, but we knew we were outnumbered by a degree.

We only found afterwards that it was by ten to one. Twenty-five thousand against our two thousand five hundred strong British and Indian force. Seeing the enemy all around us I could imagine how the defenders of Rorkes Drift[27] felt when they first caught sight of the huge contingent of Zulu warriors bearing down on them.

The word quickly passed around the ranks, not in any way an order, but advice of the most telling kind that when all hope was gone then the last round in each revolver should be reserved for self-destruction. The tales of barbaric cruelty administered by Ghazi soldiers was well-known to all of us and they delighted in slow, prolonged mutilation of those unfortunate enough to be left wounded on the battlefield. The British guns crossed the ravine and continued forward to a position where the Afghans were in range and opened fire.

The guns advanced considerably further than Burrows intended, the rest of our force hurrying up in support; the infantry in a line, with the 66th on the right, Jacob's Rifles in the centre and the 1st Grenadiers on the left. We were sitting ducks for Ayub's artillery who commanded the high ground. The first phase of the battle comprised an artillery duel; the Afghans out-shooting us, having a greater number of more modern and heavier guns, including six state-of-the-art Armstrong guns.

The 1st Grenadiers and the cavalry suffered significant casualties, while the 66th and Jacob's Rifles were able to find

---

[27]The Battle of Rorke's Drift, was a battle in the Anglo-Zulu War. The massive Zulu attacks on Rorke's Drift came very close to defeating the much smaller garrison, but were ultimately repelled. Eleven Victoria Crosses were awarded to the defenders, along with a number of other decorations and honours.

cover from the bombardment. I was already hard at work at the rear of the advance using makeshift operating tables. I wept openly for there was so little we could do. Men were dying around us from their horrific wounds before we could even move a muscle to alleviate their suffering. I truly believed that day that I would die, that we would all die and whilst doing all I could for the men under my care I was acutely aware that all I was doing was postponing death for a few hours at most.

It was the most wretched time of my life. Following the artillery exchange, the Afghan infantry massed in front of our faltering line for an assault. In a pre-emptive move, Burrows ordered the 1st Grenadiers to attack, but then cancelled the order even though the advance was making progress, fearing that the Grenadiers were suffering excessive casualties from the Afghan gunfire. It was the mark of a man who was unused to battle and seemed to have no clear idea of how to proceed.

The advance across the open plain exposed our left flank; the threat from the enveloping Afghan cavalry causing Burrows to move two companies of Jacob's Rifles to this flank and bolstering them with two of the smooth bore guns on their left, between Jacob's Rifles and the troops of the baggage guard. You understand that these details were not wholly known to me at the time, but we received snippets of how the battle was unfolding from the hordes of men who were cleared out to our medical unit. Our commanders had not realised that a hidden second ravine ran beside the force's other flank, joining the main ravine in their right rear. The Afghans used this ravine during the battle to infiltrate down our right flank, forcing the 66th Foot to wheel to face the Afghans, until the regiment faced at right angles to its neighbours, Jacob's Rifles and the 1st Bombay Grenadiers.

The degree of confusion this caused can easily be imagined. The Jacob's Rifles gave way and crumbled into the Bombay Grenadiers. All was chaos. The enemy taking advantage of this confusion were falling upon the men hacking them to pieces with their *tulwars*, a long, curved sword which inflicted the most horrible wounds.

Even now I think that they were at least granted a reasonably quick death. Even the Ghazis were too busy in the heat of the battle to spend time and effort in mutilation. There would be time enough for that later. The heat was oppressive and we were sadly lacking basic water and food supplies. Our men were dehydrated, tired and ripe for picking off. Our force was now seriously strung out, in a horse shoe formation, exposed by the abortive advance of the infantry line, with the Afghan cavalry massing on the left flank and Afghan tribesmen, infantry and guns infiltrating down the right flank, by way of the subsidiary ravine.

There was nowhere to go, no haven for those brave soldiers who fought on against overwhelming odds. In the early afternoon, the two smoothbore guns ran out of ammunition and withdrew, a move which severely unsettled the two companies of Jacobs Rifles on the left flank, already suffering from the artillery fire and the heat. With the departure of the smooth bores, the Afghan cavalry were able to infiltrate behind the British/Indian left flank. Efforts were made to counter this move with volley firing from the two companies of Jacob's Rifles, but the fire was largely ineffective, the companies inexperienced and commanded by a newly joined officer, almost unknown to his soldiers and shockingly, did not even speak their language. On our right flank, the Afghans continued to pass down the subsidiary ravine.

A move was made by troops of the Scinde Horse to attack these Afghans but the cavalry was recalled. Ayub brought two of his guns down the subsidiary ravine and commenced firing at short range, probably as short as two hundred yards, into the 1st Grenadiers. In the early afternoon, the guns ceased firing and a mass of Afghan tribesman charged the British/Indian infantry line. The two companies of Jacob's Rifles on the left fled, leaving the flank of the 1st Grenadiers wholly exposed. The Afghans cut down numbers of the Bombay Grenadiers, the Indian soldiers apparently too exhausted and demoralised to resist and who really could blame them? The guns positioned in the centre of the line fired a last salvo and withdrew in haste, the Afghans reaching within yards of the retreating guns and overwhelming the left section. Seeing the guns go, the remainder of Jacob's Rifles dissolved into the left wing of the 66th, throwing the right of our line into confusion.

We tried to move our tables and masses of wounded men further back, but they and perhaps we were too tired to contemplate it although the time for flight was approaching fast. Not approaching fast enough for the majority of the men. Burrows sent Brigadier-General Nuttall, who commanded the cavalry an order to charge the Afghans with his men, in an attempt to restore the situation. Only 150 cavalry sowars could be assembled and these men charged half-heartedly at the Afghans surrounding the Grenadiers and withdrew immediately after the contact. Burrows rode about the field attempting to bring about a further cavalry attack, but without success. Heart had all but disappeared from our troops.

The infantry fell back in two separate directions, the left wing retreating towards Mundabad, the right, comprising the 66th, the Sappers and Miners and most of the Grenadiers pushed towards the village of Khig. Many of the Grenadiers were killed during the retreat to the main ravine. The 66th, broken up by the collapse of the two Indian regiments, fell back in small fighting groups. The 66th and the Grenadiers, pursued by large numbers of Afghans, crossed the ravine into Khig, where around a hundred officers and men made a desperate last stand in a garden on the edge of the village. Overwhelmed, the survivors withdrew through Khig, with a second stand in a walled garden.

The final stand was made by eleven survivors of the 66th outside the village, two officers and nine soldiers[28]. When all hope was gone, they charged the enemy and were hacked to pieces. The remnant of the army was enabled to leave the field, the right wing of the Afghan army held off by the surviving companies of the Grenadiers, fighting until their ammunition was exhausted and then overwhelmed.

It was during this flight that a bullet struck me and I felt a searing pain in my leg. It instantly felled me and if it weren't for the actions of Murray my orderly, who threw me across his horse then I would have been at the mercy of the pursuing Afghans who of course had no notion of mercy. Those wounded whom we had to leave behind have often been on my mind throughout the years. How they must have suffered.

My mind often dwells on the horrors of that day and its aftermath. There was, it was said, ways in which the Afghan camp followers; the wives and mothers etc could bring about the slow death of our boys. Even now, I cannot bring myself to speak of it. The terrible price of war is something we all pay. I have been paying for it over and over in my darkest moments for more than fifty years.

To return: Burrows made his way through Khig, giving up his horse to a wounded officer and being rescued by a

---

[28] Immortalised in verse by William McGonagall, a poet and tragedian of Dundee who has been widely hailed as the writer of the worst poetry in the English language.

warrant officer of the Scinde Horse, seemingly unaware that the remnant of his infantry right wing was fighting to the death behind him. The escaping British and Indian troops and camp followers streamed up the road towards Kandahar, pursued by the Afghan cavalry.

During the disorganized retreat, the pursuing Afghans were held off by a squadron of the Scinde Horse, the RHA battery and the infantry from the baggage guard, although many stragglers were caught and killed, particularly the wounded. I was slipping in and out of consciousness during this desperate flight, my mind fighting between reality and unreality. The Afghans on foot were distracted by the resistance in Khig and by the Grenadiers and the opportunity to loot the British and Indian baggage. The survivors of the brigade struggled on towards Kandahar, including all the wounded souls, until they were met by a small relieving force and the Afghan cavalry withdrew.

Upwards of a thousand men were lost on that darkest of days. I was in constant pain during the journey, journey that was made in intense heat that bit into all of us. It was a thoroughly miserable time made more so by the fact that we all were aware, although myself only in my few conscious moments, that the Afghans would pursue us all the way, for emboldened by this resounding victory Ayub would surely seek to take Kandahar.

The city was besieged, but in a half-hearted kind of way and our garrison was able to comfortably keep out Ayub's men until relief arrived. While the siege was going on, I was recovering from my wounds, the bullet having been removed from my leg, and had reached the point of being able to move freely, if a little bit gingerly, around the wards when the siege ended. It was then I was struck down by enteric fever. Days came and went and I knew nothing about where one ended and another began. I was so weak at one point I was told afterwards, that my life was despaired of. I knew nothing of this. I was lost in another world. A world of dreams and nightmares. Somehow, I pulled through.

Although the physical signs of my illness had disappeared my mental state was unstable. I had seen and heard things on the battlefield I never hoped to experience again. My waking thoughts would not release me from this mental torture. I was a wreck. I spent a further week of convalescing at the base hospital in Peshawar before the Army Medical Board decided that I was to be returned to England. They cited my wounds and recent bout of enteric fever, but I think the state of my mind had been noted and was the deciding factor. I would be no more use to the Army now. My career, such as it had been, was over. I was assigned a train to take me back to Bombay, but only after another tortuous overland journey to get me back to what I termed civilisation.

I boarded the troopship *Orontes* and once more found myself in Portsmouth. Full circle. From there, the army had insisted that I book myself in at Netley for check-ups to make sure I was free from enteric fever.

A few months before I was doctoring there, full of excitement for what lie ahead. Now I was back there as a patient, a broken man and the future unknown to me. It was, on reflection, the lowest point in my life.

Once I was discharged from Netley, I spent a few days in Southsea[29]. The army had decreed I was worthy of a pension for services rendered to Queen and country. Eleven and six was scarcely a princely sum although I was also in receipt of an interim payment intended to tide me over until I

---

[29]Southsea is a seaside resort and geographic area, located in Portsmouth at the southern end of Portsea Island, Hampshire,

could make definite arrangements to ease myself back into the life of a civilian.

Before I spent too much of this sum on the south coast I decided to gravitate towards London. There, something would come up I reasoned.

Cylinder 7

I drifted in every sense of the word, of that there is no doubt. I should have been applying to various hospital boards or visiting surgeries throughout the capital in search of general practitioners who needed a partner to share their workload. But, no, I drifted.

My income was inadequate for all but a basic life, yet I sequestered myself in bars, most of which I have long forgotten in company I have long since forgotten. I was an inveterate gambler and like most of those who gamble the occasional wins convinced me that there was nothing inherently wrong in what I was doing. In such a way did I fool myself that my life was actually on an even keel when in reality I was floundering, drowning you could say.

The owners of the private hotel I resided in on the Strand were understanding when my rent was not always forthcoming on the set days. I suppose you could say I came to my senses and either I had to find cheaper rooms elsewhere, share with someone or remove myself from the capital altogether. On that very day, I was coming to that conclusion I happened to run into Stamford at the Criterion bar[30].

In spite of my worries about money I still gravitated to a bar, call it a weakness which it undoubtedly was. Recounting the episode now just reinforces the fact that my existence had become meaningless. Hah. Full circle again. It's how I feel about my life now. The perils of old age where everything is just too much damn trouble.

Stamford, as anyone who has read my chronicles of the adventures of Sherlock Holmes can tell you, had been my dresser at Barts. Over a leisurely lunch at the Holborn we brought each other up to date on our respective lives. It was only after our second bottle of wine that the subject of rooms came up and before hardly any time had gone by, we were making our way to Barts.

I am often asked whether I had an inkling that my life was going to change so dramatically. Was there a premonition of any sort? No, of course not. I was just going to meet a man who like me, was looking to economise. For all I knew, I might not like the fellow. To be honest, at that initial meeting I am not sure I did. The arrangement was a business one and Lord knows, I was not looking for a bosom friend. I was quite content in a form of solitude I had made my own notwithstanding my forays into bars where there were no friends, just acquaintances who were happy to share a drink with you, but wanted no other part of your life. And truth be told, why would they? I was hardly sparkling company.

---

[30] The Criterion Restaurant is an opulent restaurant complex facing Piccadilly Circus in the heart of London. Apart from fine dining facilities it has a bar. It is a Grade II* listed building and is in the Top 10 most historic and oldest restaurants in the world.

Ha, another circle completed…back to Barts. Those familiar buildings, familiar corridors. And, dear Lord, that same smell. Even now, I swear I can smell it. A few steps down a stone staircase and we were within touching distance of the chemical laboratory which was our destination. During this traversal of interlinked corridors Stamford had attempted to add some colour and detail to my prospective fellow lodger. I was none the wiser for it and had not an inking what this fellow Holmes did. Was he a student? Was he employed? Did he have an income? Mind you, I could hardly blame Stamford for not knowing these things.

Holmes was, as I was to find out, not especially forthcoming on such matters. The chemical laboratory was a lofty chamber, lined and littered with countless bottles. Broad, low tables were scattered about, which bristled with retorts, test-tubes, and little Bunsen lamps, with their blue flickering flames.

There was only one student in the room, who was bending over a distant table absorbed in his work. At the sound of our steps he glanced round and sprang to his feet with a cry of pleasure. "I've found it! I've found it," he shouted to my companion, running towards us with a test-tube in his hand. So, I thought, this must be him. This somewhat excitable man. "I have found a re-agent which is precipitated by haemoglobin, and by nothing else," he added, grinning inanely. Had he discovered a gold mine, greater delight could not have shone upon his features. It was hard not to beam back at him, to share in his joy whilst not having the first notion of what this statement actually meant. In fact, even when he explained it in detail a few moments later I was none the wiser. It was the same when he threw out names who had some connection with continental crime.

Although I could see how delighted he was with whatever he had discovered, I failed to grasp the significance of this test of his. Still, he seemed cordial enough and if we were to room together then I would quickly learn more about him through close study of him. I should have realised that after his opening address, where he correctly deduced that I had been in Afghanistan, that it would be he who would be doing the learning and studying as Stamford intimated at the time.

The following day we met at 221b Baker Street to inspect the rooms he had an eye on and so agreeable were they that I was moving my possessions in that very evening. Holmes appeared the following morning with an array of boxes and crates, so many that I wondered just where everything would fit. The twin tasks of unpacking and ordering the suite of rooms exactly how we wanted took the greater part of two days. Holmes had very firm ideas regarding the layout of the sitting-room and I was more than happy to fall in with his plans and ideas. He seemed to me to a fastidiously neat and tidy man in his habits. So, you can well imagine my surprise when I came down one morning, a little late admittedly, to find utter chaos. Newspapers strewn everywhere. Journals and correspondence adorning every surface. His apology was muted and possibly not sincere. He called it a quirk of his personality and the natural order of our lives would be resumed in no time at all.

My attempt to restore this order immediately was met with vehement protest, 'Leave it be, Doctor! Please!' I left the house and when I returned several hours later all was how it had been prior to the maelstrom that had descended on the sitting-room. No further apology was forthcoming, nor was the matter mentioned again. Until the next time of course.

After a few weeks I was no further forward in ascertaining what Holmes did for a living. You may wonder why I didn't simply ask him. Somehow, it wasn't the done thing. We were not what you would call friends, not then at any rate. There were no shared intimacies other than conversation at meal times. More often than not, he would be out all hours of the day and night and when we spent time together in the evening, smoking a pipe or two it was more likely that not to be in a companionable silence. That was not always the case for Holmes was often happy to impart knowledge, all kinds of knowledge. This was not knowledge as directly applied to him; I learned nothing about the man other than his interests which were many and varied. His store of facts about virtually anything was greater than I had ever seen in anyone.

But, of what use were these facts? This knowledge of crime? Of biology? Of science? He was not studying medicine, of that I was confident. Neither did he appear to have pursued any course of reading which might fit him for a degree in science or any other recognized portal which would give him an entrance into the learned world. Yet his zeal for certain studies was remarkable and within eccentric limits his knowledge was so extraordinarily ample and minute that his observations had fairly astounded me. Surely no man would work so hard or attain such precise information unless he had some definite end in view. Desultory readers are seldom remarkable for the exactness of their learning. No man burdens his mind with small matters unless he has some very good reason for doing so.

But, what reason? As some of you will recall, I made a list detailing Holmes's knowledge in many subjects and in some subjects an abject lack of knowledge. This grand scheme would I thought result in my immediate deduction of how Holmes earned his income for he surely had one. In those early weeks I imagined that my fellow lodger had fewer friends than I for while I did have one or two callers, such as Thurston for instance, Holmes had none.

Once we could say we were well and truly settled in our new home then things began to change. There was a trickle of callers to see him, the trickle turned into a flood. I quickly deduced these were not friends, the callers were from all age groups and stations of society from well-dressed city types to working girls, from cab drivers to matronly women. Obviously, they did not represent members of Holmes's family either. They were too disparate. Some stayed no longer than ten minutes, some upwards of an hour. Some called only the once, some a few times in a single week. If I were at home then I retired to my bedroom at Holmes's request for he was, as he stated, in need of privacy.

The only clue that I had as to who or what they were was that Holmes told me they were his clients. Evidently then, he was running a business of some kind, but what that business was I could not fathom. Again, I had an opportunity of asking him a point-blank question and again my delicacy prevented me from forcing another man to confide in me. I imagined at the time that he had some strong reason for not alluding to it, but he soon dispelled the idea by coming around to the subject of his own accord.

The truth, when it was revealed to me was something I had not considered. Sherlock Holmes was a consulting detective as now everyone knows. The only one of his kind in the world or so he presented to me. I doubted his word at the time, but said nothing or indeed wrote nothing of my doubts. Through the years Holmes made various statements that required the traditional pinch of salt. Untruths no, but certainly embellishments. I have been guilty myself perhaps of embellishing some of Holmes's deeds and deductions. I am only fooling myself, there is no perhaps. I exercised a certain amount of poetic licence in recording Holmes's adventures. This is not to decry the man for he was in a way, the outstanding man of his age with skills that would take many men a whole lifetime to attain. I digress once more.

Once I was let in on the secret of Holmes's profession than I was little by little allowed into his world. It certainly gave my still meaningless existence a fillip. I now found that I was involved in the world of crime as companion and helpmate to a champion of justice and life was never to be the same again. But in those initial weeks our lives for the most part moved in separate circles. We met like ships in the night in the sitting-room or upon the stairs.

Certainly, at that point there was no notion of needing each other or depending on each other. Although Holmes had this great store of knowledge and curious, even grotesque facts, most of it tumbled out, not though what may be termed normal conversation rather more like a recital of these facts. Whether this was for my education or some deeper need of Holmes to bring these things to the fore, I did not know. I still don't know.

Gradually we became closer once I became his sometime assistant and chronicler. I find myself in a quandary here for the only reason Mr. Huntley and for that matter anyone else could be remotely interested in me is because of my association with Sherlock Holmes. Applying that yardstick then, the only people interested in this story of my life are those that know and who knows, even enjoyed my chronicles of Holmes's adventures. The point then is...er...what is the point? I have lost my thread.

Ah, yes. There seems little to be gained in trying to recount minute by minute, day by day my life with Holmes. I mean, all that information is freely available to anyone via a bookshop or a public library. The best I can do is to give the listener, sorry the reader, a flavour of what it was like. I will attempt to do so as this story of my life unfolds further. Now, I simply sound pretentious and portentous.

My life has actually been a simple one as anyone who has got this far can testify. Still, Mr. Huntley demands it of me so on I will go.

Even before *A Study in Scarlet* had been published my finances were on a sounder footing for I had also been practicing as a general practitioner assisting in a practice just off the Marylebone Road. It was an ideal location for me, being an easy fifteen-minute walk and the hours and the patients were not too onerous. With my new found, well, I hesitate to call it wealth, but certainly a little more cash than of late, I elected to visit my brother once more. I had not seen him since just before I sailed to Australia. I had written occasional letters, but no replies were forthcoming. Nevertheless, I felt it my familial duty to renew contact even if I were to be rebuffed.

To my shame, I had not written to Lily, as to why, I cannot say; some kind of natural reticence? A reluctance to admit my feelings for her? Guilt at thinking of her in a romantic way after our childhood games together? Who knows? I had no doubts that she would be married by now, maybe with a growing family. Did part of me want it to be otherwise? It was, in any case, going to be a fleeting visit I had decided of maybe three days duration. The house my brother had formerly lived in now hosted a family of four who had no knowledge of my brother. Further enquiries in the town also drew a blank. Utilising the local cab service, I made my way to the Griffiths family house. At least, Josiah and Irene were in and made me feel like the prodigal son returning home.

Josiah had now retired from practice and was most gratified to hear that I had followed in his footsteps. I told him that the skeleton that he gave me was to blame! Irene bustled about in the kitchen preparing a little treat which turned out to be nothing less than the finest of high teas.

When I mentioned Lily, I saw an anxious look pass between them. Their eyes shot out a message to each other, instantly weighing whether to let me in on some deep secret.

When their news was imparted to me it turned out to be beyond anything I could have expected. 'Your brother.' Josiah said. 'Lily married your brother.' I was knocked sideways by this and struggled to speak. I was truly mystified how my dear sweet Lily could have agree to marry my uncouth, coarse and alcoholic brother. I was angry, angry at them both. Josiah and Irene tried to placate me as this rage enveloped me. I fear I shocked them to the core with my coarse language more suited as it was to my army days than their parlour.

When the red mist finally lifted, I was asked to sit, which I did while apologising profusely. I feared what was coming next, my nerves on edge, my heart beating wildly. 'John, Henry is dead. He fell heavily down the stairs after coming home drunk. Lily found him the next morning, lying there with his neck broken. I am truly sorry, John.' While Josiah recited this sad news to me, Irene was weeping uncontrollably, her face crumpled by grief. But, grief for my brother? I could hardly imagine that.

But? 'My God…Lily…why is she not here? Is she…?' 'She is well. John,' said Irene. 'She is in Carlisle still, in the same house…with her bairns.' Children? There were children. A girl and boy I was told, Charlotte and John, just four and two years old. I recall running out of the house like a madman, intent on covering the ground to Carlisle as quick as I possibly could. My brother dead. Lily, his widow. A nephew and niece.

I was unsure as to what kind of a father I would be, but I was determined to marry Lily and bring up my brother's children. By the time I was half-way to Carlisle, this happy family had a house in London where the children would go to the finest schools, their uncle would have a successful medical practice and their mother would want for nothing.

My face, when Lily opened the door, must have displayed every emotion under the sun. It's a wonder she didn't just shut it in my face as I seemed to be only capable of speaking gibberish. Rather than that course of action, she pulled me inside and we fell into each other's arms. Seated on a small couch engrossed in their own company, playing some kind of game, were two of the sweetest looking children I had ever encountered. I immediately felt there was a bond between us. As for their mother, I had so many questions I scarcely knew where to begin.

Most of all, I wanted to know how she had come to marry my brother. I could hardly qualify it as a match made in heaven nor any kind of love match yet who I was I to judge? I had spent years away and had done virtually nothing to remain in contact with those I professed to love. Through Lily's tears the whole story tumbled out. Henry had stopped drinking and had begun to reclaim his life which was anathema to the woman he lived with for she wanted no part of a sober life or a sober Henry. My brother sought for himself a respectable position and found one in Carlisle as an assistant in the parks department of the council, responsible as part of a team for the maintenance of the recreational facilities provided throughout the town and its environs.

It was in one of those parks that he ran into Lily. Naturally, they talked of old times and of me I was gratified to hear. 'He was funny, John. He was charming and so determined to turn his life around. As for you, where were you? I had heard nothing from you. You promised to come and see me when you returned from Australia.'

Her words cut me to the quick. I had no answer for her for I had made a promise to her and my failure to keep it had stung me all these years. Maybe my relationship with Adeline had soured my taste for romance. My overriding thought as I was sitting there in Lily's house was that now I had been given a chance to atone for my previous failures. 'I thought long and hard, John, when he asked me to marry him. I knew his history, but I also could see how the future could be. He was attentive and loving, everything I could have wanted in a man. In the end I said yes of course and no woman could have done more to please her man, to make him proud.'

I asked her gently, what had happened, what had changed. 'He started drinking once more two years ago and the alcohol dragged the wild side of him out, the coarse and abusive man that must have been concealed in him all this time just waiting for the proper release.' She clung to me and wept as she approached the climax of her story. 'He became violent, never to the children, but often to me. I felt his punches, his slaps. I learned how to cover up the bruises. I could not tell anyone, I felt trapped and the worst of it was that it was my fault.'

I remonstrated with her, how on earth could be her fault? Did she invite his violence to her? 'I married him, John. That's what I mean. I should have realised that sooner or later Henry would revert to his old ways. I could not tell my parents, it would be to confess my weakness twice over for they had urged me not to marry him.'

On that fateful last night, Henry had gone out carousing with his mates while Lily was left to put the children to bed. He had been in the blackest mood imaginable that day she told me and she was fearful that his mood would be even blacker on his return.

In spite of her anxiety she had fallen into a deep sleep and heard nothing of Henry's return and subsequent fall from the very top of the stairs. 'But if the children had woken? I mean…well…I suppose I mean you would have heard them, Lily.' 'They did not wake, John.' 'My point is that…' I found it hard to put my point into words, but it ran along the lines that if a mother would waken at hearing the slightest sound from her children during the night than surely the sound of a fully grown man tumbling down the stairs was scarcely less of a disturbance. Lily smiled. 'The sound of a child's cry is different, John. Surely, you must know that. I heard nothing, nothing.'

I did not press the point and we talked of happier times as we drank tea. She spoke in vague terms of resuming her career or of going home to Corbridge to her parents where she and the children would be assured of being in a happy home. I thought the time was right and I made my proposal of marriage to her. I had rehearsed in my head during the preceding few hours, what I had not allowed for was Lily's refusal of my offer. 'Dear, sweet John. We are not who we were. I am not Maid Marian, you are not Robin Hood. You are so kind to ask, but I cannot accept. I have my own life to lead. You might say I have made me bed and have to lay in it. A marriage cannot be built on the platonic love that we have always shared. There are other reasons too.'

She would not be drawn on the other reasons nor would she listen to further entreaties on my part. Her mind was made up, the answer was no and that was it. I made arrangements of a financial kind for my nephew and niece, settling a small allowance on them to be paid twice yearly into an account I would set up for them. Lily refused any such allowance for herself, but I made her promise that should she find herself in any financial hardship she would contact me immediately. As I fastened up my overcoat, she grabbed my arm and hung on for dear life. 'I am so sorry, John, for everything. You mustn't hate me.' 'I could never hate you,' I assured her. It was only when I stood on the doorstep that the true meaning of her words hit me. 'You pushed him, didn't you?' 'Yes, I pushed him. Goodbye, John.'

The door slammed shut behind me like a metaphor for that part of my life closing. All the innocence of childhood, all those good times disappeared in that instant. I was not put on this earth to be judge and jury. I could not condemn Lily for her actions any more than I could condone my brother for his. I could and would not turn her in to the authorities. She had suffered enough, we all had.

During the long train journey, I was haunted by the fact that all that happened could be lain squarely at my door. If I had kept my promise to Lily, then who knows how things would have turned out? No man is an island and the ripples we send out through our action or inaction can have the most profound effect on the lives of others.

Cylinder 8

Once back in London it took some time to recover from the events in Cumbria. I endured so many conflicting emotions, grieving for my brother chief amongst them. Not to mention the manner of his death which would plague me for years to come. Whatever my brother had become, can it be said he deserved his violent end at the hands of his wife?

I had no doubts that Lily was speaking the truth as regards the abuse she suffered at Henry's ends, but the whole mess served to sour the memory of my brother which God knows was already soured enough and also soured forever, I thought, the bond between Lily and me.

I penned her a letter reassuring her that her confession would not be broadcast to the world, that she was free to live her life as she saw fit. I reiterated that should she be in need at any time than she was to call on me. I had no wish to banish her completely from my life while knowing as a certainty that I could never, ever feel the same about her.

You may think of course that I am, ever now, reneging on my promise by mentioning this matter, but she is beyond hurt or shame now, as is my nephew. God rest their souls. This may be an appropriate juncture to bring up my own statement, which many will be aware of, that when I arrived back in England I had no kith or kin. Of course, at that time I had no idea that I had a nephew and niece and while I had no reason to doubt my brother's continuing existence I simply chose to ignore that fact. I felt truly alone and my words truly expressed my sentiments at the time.

So, I resumed my life at Baker Street with increased opportunities to assist Holmes in all manner of cases from the sublime to the almost ridiculous. From the bloodiest to the most trivial of matters. All was grist to Holmes's mill. It was a delight for me to see the man in action at such close quarters. Readers may recall the case I chronicled as 'The Resident Patient.' From very little evidence, at least as far as I or Inspector Lanner could see, Holmes skilfully constructed the whole series of events in the sequence they occurred culminating in the death of Blessington/Sutton. It was a tour-de-force that enthralled us both, a re-telling of the events that was as clear to him and subsequently us as though we had been in that room as onlookers to the grim proceedings.

That of course, was just one example of the brilliance of Holmes's deductive powers. It was never an easy task to decide which cases I would lay before the public. If I had decided to write up every case in chronological order than the public would have long tired of Sherlock Holmes and his faithful friend, Doctor Watson. Some were solved without Holmes ever moving from the sitting-room, others were so clouded in veils of diplomatic secrecy that I was not allowed to breathe a word of any such cases. Mycroft[31] saw to that. Other cases had no compelling features that would enable me

---

[31] Holmes's brother. Watson had known Holmes seven years before he learned of Mycroft's existence.

to make a fist of presenting them as any kind of adventure. Some were too tawdry, too commonplace or just plain uninteresting.

I fervently believe that the choices I made were the correct ones that showed Holmes's brilliance at its best and gave the readers a flavour of what our lives were like. I would be the first to admit it was often a strange kind of life we shared together. With Holmes's sleuthing and my doctoring there was always an irregularity to our lives with comings and goings at all times of the day and night.

This was no ordered house as dear Mrs. Hudson could have testified to, it was a house of hustle, bustle with very few quiet times. Let me qualify that: There were lean times for Holmes for cases could become scarce at any time and although he had his chemical apparatus to indulge and test his many theories, his violin for music-making and the annals of crime to immerse himself in, he was still prone to falling into what can only be described as torpor. Generally, it was of a short duration and he would become sprightly enough in no time at all. My chief worry was that such enforced inactivity would drive him back to his favoured seven-percent solution that I had weaned him off, in spite of the struggle on my part to do so. And of course, on his.

I suppose I am trying to say that there was nothing conventional about our lives, well, certainly not in Holmes's anyway. How did I see myself at the time? Part-time doctor? Part-time detective? My medical duties which certainly should have been my priority very often took a back seat to assisting Holmes. When I eventually obtained my own medical practice then at that point there were subtle changes. Oh, I still enjoyed the chase, not that there were many chases as such. Perhaps I should say I enjoyed the hunt, that is more apt an expression. But at that time, my priorities were very much the running of my practice and the care of my patients.

My involvement in Holmes's cases were of necessity lessened by quite a degree, but as my records show, Holmes was never entirely absent from my life. And what was life with Holmes really like? What was the man like? Many questions along those lines have been put to me over the years and I hope I have been consistent in my answers. Which reminds me that I have often been accused of a lack of consistency in my telling of Holmes's cases. Well, I can hardly argue the point. I was guilty of obfuscation on many an occasion, but always to my mind, in a good course. Many people needed the protection that anonymity could bring them, so I was never slow to change places and names where I thought it absolutely necessary to do so. It may have presented me with no great problem, but to others it was as though I had committed some mortal sin. The years are all wrong, I have been told. Holmes could not have been there in that year. Surely you were married by then. That couldn't have happened how you described. How could you not know that? The dates don't fit.

Believe me, I have heard it all before and my answer in a nutshell it: It was how it was. At this late juncture I daresay even I could not produce a definitive chronology of the events and cases we shared. But then, I was not writing any kind of instructive journal or a precise diary; I was producing what I liked to call adventures. So what if such re-telling of accounts threw up discrepancies? To my mind they retained the flavour of fiction notwithstanding the fact that the events I chronicled actually occurred. Even that statement may not appease those who even doubt the identities of myself and Holmes. Not only do some doubt that we even went by those names, but doubt our very existence believing everything I wrote was pure fiction. Well, I did and do exist. Sherlock Holmes was real, but sadly departed from this life.

Anyway, once more I digress and try Mr. Huntley's patience. What was Holmes really like? Was he how I described him? How was our friendship marked? He was, I suppose, like so many others. There were contradictions in his characters. He could be taciturn and even morose. But at times, high-spirited in the extreme. Often to me, he was the most delightful of companions, but I could readily see how his superior intellect might cause him to come across as just that; superior, domineering and scathing of intelligence less than his own.

But having said that, he could be the most patient of men, taking his time to draw out information from humbler members of society without once coming across as condescending or patronising. He was in essence, I believe, an inherently gentle soul, but once crossed could be a fearful enemy. There were the occasional bursts of anger, often directed at members of Scotland Yard, who had perhaps slighted him and his work in some way. He had a need to be appreciated, even admired. His susceptibility to flattery was rather more than that. He craved an audience, he needed to be seen as the best in his field. Holmes was never really half-hearted about anything. I believe he would have been at the pinnacle at any pursuit he would have cared to indulge in. He was without doubt, the most single-minded man I ever knew.

Although he was systematic, as his indexes would attest to, he was also impulsive when the mood took him. Many is the time he would leap to his feet after hours of torpor and take himself off for a walk or on a whim, visit a concert-hall where he would lose himself completely. His ability to detach himself like this even in the middle of an abstruse problem was a remarkable characteristic of the man.

He had an iron, inflexible and would brook no arguments where his work was concerned. He knew best and that was that. Yet his general disposition was one of geniality. He was extraordinarily sensitive to criticism and could mope for days when his efforts had met with harsh words or perhaps worse, indifference. Allowing for all that, he was prone to questioning his own talents and skills. He often proposed to me that his powers were on the wane even though there was scant evidence of anything of the sort. Of course, many a man may contain such contradictions or paradoxes in their character, I am sure I do, but I had never known anyone to display quite so many.

His powers of deduction particularly when applied to strangers never failed to amaze me or unnerve those who were the recipients of Holmes's analysis. I have no doubts that many would have perceived him as odd or strange. Eccentric I suppose would be an apt word. With a reputation for seeing into the minds of people it is no wonder that many felt a nervousness in his presence as though he would reveal their closely guarded secrets and of course some had secrets that they fervently wished he would not uncover.

He intimidated people without being aware of it. That reputation preceded him time and time again. Once we had both adjusted to each other's foibles than sharing rooms was easy enough. The casual reader might think that we spent our evenings in front of a blazing fire, discoursing long into the night. Truth be told, some evenings were exactly like that, but more often than not we would be taken up with our own pursuits. Some have adjudged me guilty of playing down my own intelligence to elevate Holmes's own, leaving me at the mercy of those who would proclaim me simple or stupid. To those I would say that I knew full well the level of my own intellect and I reckoned it to be not too far below that of Holmes. My education and subsequent career in doctoring should dispel the idea that I was in some way slow-witted. Certainly, I may not have been able to deduce what Holmes could in any given situation, but then I would say that ninety percent of the population may have similarly floundered.

Another point that is worth making is that why would a man like Holmes with his undoubted brilliance saddle himself with a friend who could not reciprocate fully his friendship? Such theories do not hold up under scrutiny. As colleagues, I was in his shadow, but as friends we were equals. Comrades.

We argued of course because we had opposing views on many subjects. No friendship is ever all sunlight. Harsh words passed between us on occasion, it would have been unnatural had they not in such a long association, but our comradeship was never under threat. You could say that we rubbed along quite nicely together.

And then of course Mary Morstan entered my life. I have no need to check my notes or my published works to recall my description of her: Miss Morstan entered the room with a firm step and an outward composure of manner. She was a blonde young lady, small, dainty, well gloved, and dressed in the most perfect taste. There was, however, a plainness and simplicity about her costume which bore with it a suggestion of limited means. The dress was a sombre greyish beige, untrimmed and unbraided and she wore a small turban of the same dull hue, relieved only by a suspicion of white feather in the side. Her face had neither regularity of feature nor beauty of complexion, but her expression was sweet and amiable, and her large blue eyes were singularly spiritual and sympathetic. In an experience of women which extends over many nations and three separate continents, I have never looked upon a face which gave a clearer promise of a refined and sensitive nature. Mary was ever quick to point out that I had neglected to call her beautiful. Which she was.

Once I had managed to get over my surprise that Miss Morstan had accepted my proposal of marriage then I could, or rather we could, start planning our future together. This, obviously, would not entail us living at 221b. I fear such an arrangement would have permanently upset Holmes's equilibrium. I had recently been involved in running old Mr. Farquhar's practice in Paddington and when the opportunity arose to purchase it, I jumped at the chance. The living accommodation was ideal for a couple and the income it would afford us both, although not being a fortune, would suffice for the two of us.

I played no great part in many of Holmes's adventures for the extent of my married life for the obvious reason of being wrapped up completely in my own domestic contentment. I described it as being master of my own household and by that I meant that at long last I had a stability in my life that had hitherto mostly been hidden from me. Mary and I were partners in life and in business, both the Paddington practice and the one in Kensington that we acquired. I was no more her actual master than she was mine. It was a true union founded on true love and friendship.

Holmes was not entirely absent from our lives and Mary was ever willing to excuse my absences when Holmes had need of me, for she expressed a great fondness for Holmes and in turn he was complimentary towards her being impressed by her intelligence and according her the greatest accolade, for him anyway, of having all the makings of a detective herself. Holmes being the man he was, could not see the benefits that romantic love can bring. The very idea of a having a wife or paramour was anathema to him. His single-minded approach to his profession would be severely compromised by such personal detours. I lived in hope however that Cupid's arrow would one day find its way to him. A false hope of course.

Shortly before the wedding I felt I had a duty to write to Lily to invite her and my niece and nephew to share this happy event with me. I had no great wish to see her, the revulsion I felt when hearing her revelation of killing my brother had never really left me although God knows I understood it and in a way, I was not apportioning blame to her for her action. It's just that my feelings had necessarily changed and I would never be able to divorce the woman from her act. I had written occasional letters asking after health and schooling etc., to some of these I received a reply, to some I did not. The wedding invitation was met with silence. Of the friends, few admittedly, that I had made, only Thurston was able to attend and handled the best man duties admirably.

My, it was such a happy time in my life. My good fortune at finding a wife that possessed so many fine qualities was everything to me. My life was given over completely to making Mary happy. I hope that could she have a say now that she would reckon that I succeeded in my ambition. She was of such a sweet and sympathetic nature that folks that were in grief came to her like birds to a lighthouse. My blessings were indeed overflowing.

During the early years of my marriage Holmes had been very busy indeed, his fame now taking him all over Europe some cases involving various royal families. Other cases at this time were more down to earth such as the Dundas separation case, the Darlington substitution scandal and the extraordinary case involving Colonel Warburton's madness. Some of these cases, I wrote up notes for, but none found their way into the published chronicles.

Even now, I have these notes and if I have the energy, for I decidedly have the time, I may well set down some of these cases in a new volume. The giant rat of Sumatra will not feature, even at this late pass I still feel it is a story for which the world is still not prepared.

This period of contentment was fast approaching its curtain call although I had no inkling of it. Everything was resolutely normal. Those who have followed the exploits of Sherlock Holmes will be very familiar with the events I chronicled as The Final Problem. I am convinced that the only people interested in my life as I am telling it now will be those self-same folk who only know of me through my efforts as Holmes's biographer so once more I do not propose to relate chapter and verse as that information is freely available elsewhere.

Damn, I may be repeating myself. More editing work for Mr. Huntley! The mad dash to the continent, the pursuit by Moriarty, the final meeting and death of Holmes and Moriarty at the Reichenbach Falls…all this will be familiar. The grief I felt as I travelled back to England was acute. I blamed myself for not being there when he needed me most, for being taken in so easily thus leaving the way clear for Moriarty to launch his murderous assault. Mary was on hand to nurse me through this dark time, to help restore my shattered nerves. I fancied in my darkest moments that I could hear Holmes's screams as he plummeted to his death. I was haunted by my failure to protect the best and wisest man I had ever known. I consoled myself by continuing to write up adventures from my copious notes; in this way I could keep Holmes alive by acting as his living memorial.

With Mary's ministrations I was able to return to my normal self and the practice continued to thrive. The shadow, I reckoned, had gone from our lives. I was not overly worried when Mary fell ill with a heavy cold which quickly turned into influenza, she had always been susceptible to colds and coughs. The cough she now developed became persistent in its nature and she was an abject creature when wracked by bouts of coughing that would render her so weak. Tuberculosis. I knew it and she knew it.

We discussed how our lives would be altered. We did not countenance death while there was a chance for survival. The practice was put into abeyance with locums operating a slimmed down surgery. There was evidence that fresh air and a changed diet could reverse the consumptive symptoms, mountain air was particularly recommended. Ironically, we made our way to the mountains of Switzerland where tragedy had already infused my life.

The journey was uncomfortable, painful and interminable. Mary remained wrapped up, swaddled in layers of clothing and isolated from other passengers. The romantic poets sought to find beauty in the horror and melancholy of consumption. There was certainly horror and melancholy, but no beauty in a disease that ravaged so many.

In the mountains, at a small clinic that was run more along the lines of a holiday resort, patients were encouraged to walk as much as possible to enable fresh air from all quarters of the compass to enter their lungs. At first, Mary could only manage a few steps, but gradually as she strengthened she was able to manage a good few miles a day. After a few weeks spent thus, she was involved in some form of outdoor exercise for upwards of eight hours a day.

Coupled with a strict regimen of three healthy meals a day, this made for remarkable changes within her. I clung to the hope that she was cured and therefore saved whilst being very aware that sooner or later the disease could yet strengthen its hold on her. Yet, the journey back to England was so different from the outward journey. Mary was brighter although still weak. I was overjoyed to see colour in her cheeks now replacing the deathly pallor of just a few weeks ago. My joy was short-lived. There were to be no more periods of remission. Mary deteriorated quickly, so quickly in fact that another proposed trip to Switzerland had to be cancelled for Mary was far too weak to travel.

I barely strayed from her side in those final days, her emaciated frame rendered her almost unrecognisable from how she looked when she entered the sitting-room of 221b just five years before. The end when it came was mercifully quick and Mary slipped away from me one cold, dark morning. I continued to hold her hand as I had been doing for several hours. I squeezed it as if that very act could bring her back to life. Almost at once I began to experience the debilitating effects of being *alone* and *incomplete*. The sense of feeling like you have lost an essential part of yourself is both painful and disconcerting. The world suddenly looked like a different place, often odd and distanced. I was no longer sure how to cope with life in general, and sometimes I wondered if I even wanted to try.

The reality was that I had no one to turn to and I desperately needed someone. The opportunity to talk about the Mary, her life as well as her death, what I missed about her, my feelings of loneliness, anger and many others, and to review the final days of our life and relationship was denied to me. Oh, friends like Thurston offered support and continuing friendship, but they were not people I could open up to.

Even Mycroft Holmes, in a rare departure from his precise routine called upon me to offer his condolences. The days that followed Mary's death were both utterly full and completely empty…full of activity that had to be accomplished for I still had a living to earn, yet empty of life. Much of the time I sleepwalked through the things I had to do, so numb that I was often completely unaware of what was going on around me. I felt cut off from everything that I thought was my life. Then an event or a few spoken words would bring me out of my darkness, only to find myself standing alone and confused on some strange and unfamiliar street, full of feelings and memories, but also feeling utterly lost.

Everything I did involved a great effort on my part, forcing myself to dress, forcing myself to bathe, to work. Gradually, without even realising it, a semblance of normality returned. The phrase 'life must go on' is much touted, but in essence it is true. There was also a realisation that Mary would have been appalled by the wreck of a man I had become.

I threw myself into my doctoring, I once more began to read the newspapers to feel connected to the outside world. Not surprisingly given my association with Sherlock Holmes, I scoured reports of crime particularly if there seemed to be some elements which lifted such crimes out of the commonplace and into the mysterious. Reading between the lines of some of these, I attempted to apply Holmes's methods in a modest way to see whether I could glean anything extra from these reports that might guide me toward a solution. However, I was not as adept as I imagined myself to be at sleuthing from a distance.

There was none, however, which appealed to me like this tragedy of Ronald Adair. As I read the evidence at the inquest, which led up to a verdict of wilful murder against some person or persons unknown, I realised more clearly than I had ever done the loss which the community had sustained by the death of Sherlock Holmes.

There were points about this strange business which would, I was sure, have specially appealed to him and the efforts of the police would have been supplemented, or more probably anticipated, by the trained observation and the alert mind of the first criminal agent in Europe. All day as I drove upon my round I turned over the case in my mind, and found no explanation which appeared to me to be adequate. The opening words of 'The Empty House' still thrill me because of what they would lead to. But that is a story for the next cylinder and a new morning. I feel excessively tired.

Cylinder 9

Mary featured in my dreams of last night. My remembrances of yesterday brought her back into focus. She had not inhabited a dream of mine for many years. So many memories still here in my admittedly fading memory.

The murder of Ronald Adair and the return of Sherlock Holmes, that's where I must start today. My reaction to Holmes's return has a tendency to puzzle people. Why I did not rant and rage at his devious and harmful subterfuge in hiding the fact that he was still living? Why did I immediately fall in with assisting him? Over forty years on and I feel compelled to explain. What I described was an immediate reaction of mine to his sudden appearance.

The friendship we had forged was at the forefront of my mind and I was, as I stated, overjoyed to see him alive and standing in front of me. Those emotions crowded out others which would bubble to the surface only later. Chief among these was my anger, unreasonable the fact of it may be, that Holmes was alive yet Mary was dead. I, of course, was not blaming Holmes for her death, but I grieved in differing ways for both of them. If Holmes could be re-born, why not Mary? Yes, irrational I know.

Now, what I have to say may sound like heresy to some, but that emotional reunion with Holmes was not in reality quite how I depicted it. Yes, I was amazed to see him which is not quite the same as being overjoyed. The sequence of events then differed somewhat. I demanded a full explanation of what had driven him to allow me to believe he was dead. Of why he could treat a trusted friend and comrade that way. His explanation after I fainted that he had no idea I would be so affected was particularly hurtful. Then the other side of the coin was that in front of me was a man who had a peculiar difficulty in allowing emotions to alter his equilibrium. He really had no idea of what troughs of despair his 'death' would bring about in me.

That we were able to continue our friendship was a miracle itself, but at that stage of my life I realised how much I needed Holmes in my life. In some ways we came to be dependent on each other although I very much doubt that he would have admitted to such a dependency. But, as history records, I joined with Holmes in the capture of Colonel Sebastian Moran and before too long found myself back in my old quarters. Once more assisting Holmes whilst keeping my doctoring hand in even after selling the Kensington practice for a very good price indeed. History also records how that transaction came about.[32]

The year following on from Holmes's return was one of the busiest of his career. The cases came thick and fast with barely time to draw breath. The majority of these cases remain unchronicled. The best I could do was to acknowledge these cases in passing which even then

---

[32] A relative of Holmes purchased the practice, the money to do so evidently coming from Holmes.

infuriated people who reckoned I was just teasing them with these tantalising glimpses of adventures that would never be told. Perhaps I was. Perhaps I did so deliberately.

The pre-eminence that Holmes had achieved in his chosen profession before the three-year hiatus had not noticeably been diminished in his absence and now had risen to even greater heights. I personally believe that around that time he was at the peak of his powers. Not that I mean that there was any falling off of his skills in the latter years of his career, more that his talents were seen at their best during those post-hiatus years. His mental and physical form were seen to their best advantage and he was called upon by all and sundry, even his Holiness the Pope[33].

By comparison, 1896 was a barren year when for whatever reason, the great cases failed to materialise. Of course, there were some cases that Holmes looked into, but on the whole the first few months of the year were punctuated by Holmes bemoaning the fact of enforced idleness that he had to suffer. And when Holmes suffered, I suffered too I can tell you!

That was all to change when I received a letter from my old friend, Godfrey Jacobs, who I believe I have mentioned before in my ramblings. The letter extended an invitation for me to visit him and his family in Lyme Regis on the Dorset coast. Much to my surprise, Holmes after a spot of cajoling on my part, elected to travel with me. Almost immediately when we arrived at that docile, peaceful spot then we were embroiled in a mystery, the like of which we had never known. Rather like the giant rat of Sumatra it is a tale for which the world is unprepared, the stuff of nightmares and dreams. Belief systems counted for nothing

---

[33] An unchronicled case involving the sudden death of Cardinal Tosca.

during that time and if you agree that faith is defined as something that enables us to believe things that we know to be untrue, then we had faith a-plenty.

I will say only this, that I the most flat-footed of men faced head on a force I did not understand. Holmes that most scientifically minded of men saw for himself something that science could not explain. I did commit an account to paper of the nature of what we encountered in Lyme, but it is not an account for the consumption of the general public nor will it ever be so.[34]

Amongst the dark horror we encountered was a chink, no, more than a chink of light for I met a widow, Mrs Beatrice Heidler who captured my heart when I doubted it would ever be captured again. I suffered when I recognised my feelings for her. I suffered through guilt. Guilt at loving again when Mary had been at rest for only four years. I felt I was being untrue to her, to her memory. Yet, I could not fight the feelings that were growing for Beatrice, nor did I wish to. My feelings were reciprocated to my joy and we made plans to be together. Beatrice had a sixteen-year-old son, Nathaniel and she, quite rightly, did not want to uproot him. Instead we agreed to wait until he had come of age before we could marry and be together fully.

In consequence, I travelled frequently to Lyme Regis over the coming years and left Holmes to his own devices although I was on hand to assist quite often in spite of his dark mutterings about my imminent desertion of him. Holmes himself had occasion to further visit Lyme too. For such a beautiful resort, it had its share of bizarre crime that fortunately we were on hand to deal with, one featuring an adversary from the past bent on vengeance against

---

[34] Watson's papers came to light and the account was published in 2009 as 'Sherlock Holmes and the Lyme Regis Horror'.

us.[35] During that episode, Beatrice was abducted and held hostage and her very life threatened. It was the most harrowing of times with Beatrice adding bravery to her already formidable talents. Again, this case and a further episode in that loveliest of spots in Dorset will have to remain unpublished.

On the whole,1897 proved to be another slow year and as always, at such times I was ever careful and watchful in case Holmes should slip back to his usage of artificial stimulants. A veritable flurry of cases greeted the opening months of the year however and even Holmes's iron constitution began to wilt under the pressure of sustained hard work coupled with a poor diet and lack of sleep. A sabbatical was sought and a trip to Cornwall was the favoured prescription. Life was never that simple though and once again we were plunged into another puzzle.[36]

Some of the following years were more memorable by the failures rather than successes. I should qualify my use of the word failure as they were not cases where Holmes had all the facts at his disposal and then failed to find a solution, but rather affairs he looked into that revealed no clues whatsoever as to the unravelling the answers as to what had occurred. I am particularly reminded of the case of Mr. James Phillimore, who, stepping back into his own house to get his umbrella, was never more seen in this world. We spent two hours in Phillimore's house seeking a solution and came away as puzzled as when we had arrived. 'We know only too well, Watson, do we not, that there are incidents that remain outside of our understanding? This may run along similar

---

[35] From Watson's papers it can be learned that this adversary was Stapleton of Hound of the Baskerville fame and this new affair ended in Stapleton's death (finally!) on Dartmoor.
[36] The Adventure of the Devil's Foot.

lines,' Holmes said as we exited the house in an oblique reference to our first visit to Lyme Regis.

We also looked into the case of Isadora Persano, the well-known journalist and duellist, who was found stark staring mad with a match box in front of him which contained a remarkable worm said to be unknown to science. Poison was suspected, but there were no obvious signs of how that could be administered. There were no signs of madness in his forebears, nothing to suggest that he was liable to become a victim of the complete loss of his senses. The worm itself was removed to an entomology department at the zoo where the following morning it had disappeared completely. Mystery upon mystery with no answer.

Holmes, rather surprisingly, took these setbacks in his stride, complaining only to me that he was not the magician I made him out to be. Of course, he had a point for my goal in initially bringing these adventures before the public was to put Holmes the detective, where he should rightly be, recognised and admired by all for his superior intellect and sleuthing skills and I could hardly do that by trumpeting to everyone his failures. In essence, I was guilty as charged!

I am racking my brains regarding what I have so far recorded on these cylinders to see whether I have dealt Mrs. Hudson the ultimate injustice of not mentioning her. I believe I have...damn...why can't I remember that when I remember so much about the events of over thirty years ago? If I have failed her, let me redress that now.

Mrs. Hudson, was what I would describe as a feisty woman, given to outbursts of righteous indignation. And, believe me, she could do righteous indignation like no other. But, good-hearted, kind-hearted and when not in the grips of an outburst, quite long-suffering. When dealing with a lodger like Sherlock Holmes patience is a necessary virtue and whilst she possessed it, she didn't always display it. When

Holmes found himself in a battle of wills with her, it was always he who backed down, she could be fearsome in an argument. She was proud of us, I knew that. She treated us like her property, as an extension of her house. It was almost as though we belonged to her. Doughty, feisty, yet gentle. I thought her magnificent. I mentioned the battle of wills between her and Holmes which put me in mind of boxers circling each other, looking for weaknesses to exploit.

On occasions like that it would be easy to assume there was no love lost between them, but it was no surprise to me that when Holmes retired to the Sussex coast, Mrs. Hudson promptly sold the Baker Street house and retired with him. 'To look after him,' she said, but I am of the mind it was to look after one another.

But, I get ahead of myself again. Around the turn of the century, Holmes began to talk of retirement. I had no notion that he was even contemplating such an action. He was under the belief that his powers were on the wane. I saw no evidence of that and told him so. He was still very much in demand and recent triumphs as we headed into a new century would ensure that would remain so. The Adventure of the Six Napoleons was one such triumph. Not only did it spark a fulsome vote of thanks from Lestrade, it also revealed how Holmes could be snared himself by the softer emotions. I could not recall Holmes ever being so moved as he was when Lestrade revealed how everyone at Scotland Yard from the lowest to the highest was proud of him. It may have been a flickering emotion, a momentary slipping of the mask, but it was there, I saw it.

I was to see it again two years later. Holmes's determination to retire was reinforced when he received a huge reward in the shape of a £12,000 fee from the Duke of Holdernesse. This, I believe, was the final catalyst in making his mind up, this unexpected plume in his finances suddenly gave him both the funds and the reason to draw his career to a close. Not that he wasn't a comparatively wealthy man before that despite his protestations to the Duke that he was a poor man. His profession had brought him fame and wealth and that was true for me also albeit in a more modest way.

While he was busy arranging his escape to the Sussex downs there were still a few cases which came our way although he was becoming more and more selective in his selection of which problems to look into. And of course, I was busy with arrangements of my own with an impending marriage to look forward to and the proposed acquisition of a practice in Queen Anne Street.

It seemed that the end of our dwelling and sleuthing together would dovetail nicely, but that wasn't the case. It was directly after the 'Three Garridebs' case that Beatrice and I were married. This took place in Lyme Regis on an early summer's day where the fates had conspired to grant us the most beautiful of days on which to be wed. Holmes travelled down with me and was the most attentive of wedding attendants with barely any muttering under his breath regarding the futility of romance. It was during the 'Three Garridebs' investigation that I truly saw Holmes's heart. I recorded it such:

In an instant he had whisked out a revolver from his breast and had fired two shots. I felt a sudden hot sear as if a red-hot iron had been pressed to my thigh. There was a crash as Holmes's pistol came down on the man's head. I had a vision of him sprawling upon the floor with blood running down his face while Holmes rummaged him for weapons. Then my friend's wiry arms were round me, and he was leading me to a chair. "You're not hurt, Watson? For God's sake, say that you are not hurt!" It was worth a wound—it was worth many wounds—to know the depth of loyalty and love which lay behind that cold mask. The clear, hard eyes were dimmed for a moment, and the firm lips were shaking. For the one and only time I caught a glimpse of a great heart as well as of a great brain. All my years of humble but single-minded service culminated in that moment of revelation. "It's nothing, Holmes. It's a mere scratch." He had ripped up my trousers with his pocketknife. "You are right," he cried with an immense sigh of relief. "It is quite superficial." His face set like flint as he glared at our prisoner, who was sitting up with a dazed face. "By the Lord, it is as well for you. If you had killed Watson, you would not have got out of this room alive."

I questioned Holmes as to this statement of intent, doubting that in the cold light of day and reason that he would follow it through or even be capable of following it through. He assured me that it was exactly what would have happened I had not survived, 'he had forfeited his life, Watson and I would have had no compunction regarding taking it.'

Prior to my nuptials, I felt duty bound to send yet another invitation to Lily. I realised of course that the journey from Carlisle to the Dorset coast would be out of the question for her, but nevertheless I felt compelled from a familial necessity. It was now fifteen years since I had last seen her and the children. The children were no longer children now, Charlotte being nineteen and James seventeen. There had been fitful correspondence between us and as each volume of stories was published I made sure to send my niece and nephew handsomely bound copies for which I received due acknowledgement. In the intervening years, Lily had forsaken teaching for nursing, the shift patterns being better for bringing the children up. Whether she had entered into another romance I did not know. Being a beautiful woman, I am sure there would have been no lack of suitors, particularly as Charlotte and James became more independent.

Both had finished their schooling, Charlotte electing to follow her mother into nursing and James favouring a career in the army. Shades of their uncle! Being my only kith and kin, I should have made the time to travel north to visit them. I prevaricated and stalled; the reality was that I had not formulated a way to approach Lily again after our last parting. Weakness on my part I know, but there it was.

God, how to explain it? Without seeing her, I could still, just about anyway, think of her as my Maid Marian of old and the young woman who bade me farewell as I took myself off to Australia. If I saw her, the remembrance of my last visit would cloud my vision of her, no longer Maid Marian, but my brother's killer. Even so, I resolved to take the trip to Carlisle to see her and introduce Beatrice as were planning a trip to Scotland. Perhaps that way, I could lay that particular demon to rest.

1903 began for Holmes with a commission from the Sultan of Turkey, with consequences of the direst kind for the whole of Europe if he should fail. He did not confide in me and supply the details or the ramifications of the case, but after two months work he declared the matter over and the result was exactly the one that the Sultan had sought. I was almost entirely caught up with my Marylebone [37]practice in which Beatrice was the perfect helpmate. I had not thought to experience such domestic bliss again in my lifetime, once Mary had passed I was convinced I would never love again. The fact I could and did was a constant source of amazement to me. I was fortunate enough to know the love of two good women and my life was immeasurably enriched by the experience. I can heartily recommend it!

---

[37] The site of Watson's Queen Anne Street practice is now occupied by the Queen Anne Street Medical Centre.

By the end of the year, Holmes had finally put his affairs in order and decamped to the Sussex downs. Once Mrs. Hudson had completed the sale of dear old 221b and put her own affairs in order, she followed. After Holmes had viewed many properties, he settled on a villa just inland with glorious views over the channel.[38] Prior to his departure we spent a long evening together in that sitting-room which had seen the start of so many adventures. We reminisced, we laughed, we re-visited both solved cases and unsolved cases; we spoke of sadness we had both suffered, of ambition, of life and everything under the sun. It was quite like old times. Twenty-two years on, our partnership was finally dissolved. Or so I thought.

---

[38] In the village of Fulworth, East Sussex.

Cylinder 10

I saw little of Holmes from that time forward although I made sporadic visits to Sussex together with Beatrice. I fully expected him to return to his profession rather than stagnate amongst his bees and bucolic views which surely would pale before long. I was mistaken.

Sherlock Holmes was perfectly at home there on the downs as though it had always been his life. He rarely came to town and even though he had requests for help from Scotland Yard, their entreaties came to nothing. Even a direct call for assistance from the prime minister and the cabinet came to nothing. The man who had done so much sterling work in Scarborough just the year before, unmasking a spy at the heart of government was not the same man; his solitude was now sacrosanct to him. I was certainly not contemplating retirement, being as busy as I had ever been.

Without the diversions that life with Holmes meant, I was throwing myself into my medical career with new vigour. New advances in diagnosis and treatments were coming thick and fast and just keeping abreast of those was a full-time occupation in itself. I also had the great fortune to become an honorary grandfather when Nathaniel, Beatrice's son, and his wife, Elizabeth became parents. Rose grew to be a fine young lady who had made her career on the stage and more recently in the cinema where she had certainly made a name for herself. I always attend her opening nights and for her part, she is always pleased to see me. She visits me often, the one remaining link with my life outside of these walls, outside of my memories.

Once again, I race on a little, I must keep ordered. Even in those early years of the century there were storm clouds gathering in Europe, the political alliances designed to keep the peace were constantly being pulled and twisted one way or another. Diplomacy could only go so far in keeping warring factions at bay, but at the time no one really thought that a war would become a reality. Surely, no monarch or government would allow that to come about, after all most of the ruling heads of Europe were related to one another.

The Scottish trip that Beatrice and I had discussed if not actually planned eventually took place in 1906. It was to be a welcome break for us, after years of unrelenting hard work. I wrote a letter to Lily informing her that we would break our journey in Carlisle and pay her a visit. To my shame, I had not told Beatrice the full story of Lily and Henry other than the fact they were man and wife and Henry had met with an unfortunate accident. Once I had revealed the truth then she was most understanding as I knew she would be. Before I had a reply from Lily, not that I was really sure whether I would get one, my nephew turned up on our doorstep. This was the first time I had clapped eyes on him since he was two years old. Now he was a strapping young man of twenty-six, confident and outgoing and so much like his father that I involuntarily winced when he stood before me in my study. One of the reasons that he was here, the chief reason really was to know more about his father. What kind of man was he? What kind of father? What kind of husband?

I felt it my duty to protect him from the excesses of his father without being too sure of what Lily had told him. Oh, I knew of course that she would not have told James of the actual circumstances of his father's death. She may have even presented a sanitised version of Henry's life. He wasn't exactly forthcoming, so I did what I could for him. I explained that his father and I had not always seen eye to eye, even from an early age. However, I took great care not to blacken Henry's character too much, stressing that he had evidently loved Lily and his two children. I had no idea whether that was strictly true, but I have never been averse to bending the truth here and there, in spite of Holmes accusing me of not being able to dissemble. James seemed satisfied with my portrayal of his father and if I was expecting any awkward questions, I was relieved to have none to answer.

He was also eager to learn of my military adventures as he had seen action himself during the Second Boer War. He was inordinately proud of his actions during this conflict and was mentioned in dispatches for his bravery under fire at Pieter's Hill[39] and also at Bridle Drift[40]. It was clear to me that the military was his life and he was taking every opportunity to further his career with promotion coming quickly through the ranks.

---

[39] Part of The Battle of Tugela (or Thukela) Heights, consisted of a series of military actions lasting from 14 February through 27 February 1900 in which General Sir Redvers Buller's British army forced Louis Botha's Boer army to lift the Siege of Ladysmith during the Second Boer War.

[40] Part of the Battle of Colenso, 15th December 1899.

My own experience of over twenty-five years before could still give me the odd sleepless night. The nightmares, once so prominent, had dwindled, but still had the power to put me squarely back in the thick of the battle. Even now, the horror of that day can come back to haunt me. Charlotte, he told me, was now a staff sister in the Manchester Hospital for Skin Diseases, a brand-new hospital[41] in the Salford area of the city. She was determined to be the most efficient nurse there, evidently being as single-minded as her brother, not a trait they inherited from my brother in any shape or form. Both of them remained single although James spoke in glowing terms of a young lady named Constance who hailed from Penrith, but he would not be drawn further.

As unexpected visits go, not that they were common in my life, it was a great joy to be reunited with my nephew and we vowed to keep in touch. He gave me an address of the nurse's quarters in Quay Street for Charlotte and I wrote to her and extended an open invitation to her to come and visit when she had a break from her duties. In fact, it was to be nine years before I saw Charlotte, well, before I met both of them again and in such terrible circumstances. Once more, I race on ahead. I obtained from James, a new address in Carlisle for Lily, a small cottage which adjoined the hospital where she worked as a matron. I therefore wrote another letter advising her of our impending trip to Scotland and our desire to call on her. I received in return a brief note saying that should she happen to be at home on the date I had suggested than we would be most welcome to call.

Well, we broke our northward journey in Carlisle on the appointed day and made our way to Lily's cottage. Our knocks met with no answer. We called at the hospital, expecting to find she had been called in to work, but we were

---

[41] It opened in May 1906.

informed that she had taken the day off, citing family business. We tried the cottage once more, a futile act I knew as I could see that she had decided against seeing us. To be honest, I was not sure what I would have to say to her after all this time so perhaps it was a blessing in disguise that she had made the plans she had. I scribbled a note and put through her door, expressing the disappointment that I *should* have felt at her absence. Our Grand Tour of Scotland came to an end six weeks later and once more we threw ourselves back into work.

My routine was thus: five days a week I spent in my consulting office, two evenings, if required, in home visits and two evenings a week filing and continuing to write up some of Holmes's cases despite various injunctions he tried to place upon me. Holmes may have been physically in Sussex, but his presence in my life was constant. I received a stream of missives from the man which alternated between downright ordering me not to write of his career ever again to suggesting some adventures that he thought would suit my pen. Even now, I have the notes of over one hundred cases which, although entirely suitable for publication, will now never see the light of day. I do not have the strength left to see such projects through. It's possible of course that in the future someone may take up the mantle of Holmes's biographer and bring these tales to the public.

Equally so, it may be that both Holmes and I will be largely forgotten in the future. Time will tell, time that I have so little of. By 1910 I was entertaining thoughts of retirement myself, the practice was worth a pretty penny and I was fortunate enough to be the recipient of royalties on a regular basis. Beatrice was very supportive of this notion of mine and we started to work towards that goal. 1914 was the mooted year this would come about and the idea was to retire to Dorset and naturally to Lyme Regis.

Outside of our domesticity however there were dark clouds enveloping Europe. There was talk of war, but then there was always talk of war, but this time the voices were nagging and insistent. The European powers, despite the treaties which bound so many of them together, were making threatening noises and it was feared that none of these treaties would go very far in preventing war. No matter that most of the ruling heads were related, that appeared to make little difference as the tension mounted. Britain objected to the moves Germany was making to increase its army and found Germany's attempt to colonise parts of Africa particularly objectionable. This of course in spite of the British Empire accounting for a quarter of the world.

Allied to this growing militarism was an intense nationalism in most of the Great powers. Weltpolitik or the desire for world power status was very popular in Germany. The French desire for revenge over Alsace and Lorraine was very strong. In Britain Imperialism and support for the Empire was very evident. The likelihood of war increased with every passing day. That fateful day in Sarajevo[42] was the trigger that realised everyone's fears. War was upon us.

Shortly before war had been declared, I had accepted a handsome offer for the Queen Anne Street practice. This time, the money had not arrived after a circuitous route from Holmes! The plan, long spoken about, was as I may have mentioned, to retire to the Dorset coast, but the outbreak of hostilities altered those plans. I had no desire at all to once more enter the theatre of war, but I felt I had a duty to King and country to make myself available.

I must backtrack a little here for as some of you will know, 1914 was the year when I was once more involved in a case with Holmes if only in the sense I was in at the kill.

---

[42] The assassination of Arch-Duke Ferdinand.

Holmes, at that time had almost passed beyond my ken. I had scarcely seen the man for over two years. Out of the blue I received a wire asking me to meet him at Harwich[43] with a car. 'A car, my dear?' I exclaimed to Beatrice. 'Where the deuce does he expect me to obtain a car? And how on earth do I ensure it reaches that port?'

Beatrice smiled sweetly at me, 'I rather think, John, that he is expecting you to drive it.' Up to that point I had remained superbly uninterested in motor vehicles. I did not wish to drive one or own one. Not that I was a Luddite[44] on the quiet. I knew motor-cars had a future, indeed they were the future, but just not my future...or present. As ever, when bidden by Holmes, I applied myself to the task in hand.

I paid over the odds I feel for a Ford Model T which I was assured by the salesman, was the easiest car to drive. Holmes had informed me that any expenses involved would be reimbursed by a grateful government so at least my purse was safe even it my nerves were about to be shredded by my own somewhat erratic driving skills. I had only been to Harwich three times previously and it is fair to say that it had never figured on my list of the top one hundred English towns to visit. Not that I had ever formulated such a list.

It is equally fair to say that never had I felt such a warmth and affection for the town as I did that late afternoon when I was proud to say I had made it in one piece. Did the experience of travelling north on the A12 bring about a reconciliation between myself and the motor-car? No, after that episode I never went near another blessed car.

---

[43]Harwich is a town in Essex, England and one of the Haven ports, located on the coast with the North Sea to the east.

[44] A person opposed to increased industrialization or new technology.

It was remarkable to see how little Holmes had changed since I had last seen him. Beatrice was convinced he lived on a diet of Royal jelly and fully expected him to live until he was one hundred and fifty! The only change I could see was Holmes's face was now adorned with a small goatee which did nothing for him whatsoever. I gathered it was some manner of disguise which he confirmed for me as he related what manner of work he had been undertaking for the last two years at the express request of the government. A passing thought at the time was that surely a government department could have supplied a car and driver without me having to risk life and limb, but there was a pleasing symmetry that if this promised to be Holmes's last case then it was an act of sentiment and friendship that had caused him to wire me.

The events of that evening whereby the German agent, Von Bork was captured are well known to the public through the publication of His Last Bow. I took the unusual step of telling the story as a third-party narrator for I was only present at the finale as it were. I may have taken one or two liberties in re-imagining certain conversations, but it was absolutely necessary to bring Holmes's last case before the public. Holmes's words to me as we stood on the terrace that evening still bring a tingle to my spine. 'There's an east wind coming, Watson.' 'Good old Watson! You are the one fixed point in a changing age. There's an east wind coming all the same, such a wind as never blew on England yet. It will be cold and bitter, Watson, and a good many of us may wither before its blast. But it's God's own wind none the less, and a cleaner, better, stronger land will lie in the sunshine when the storm has cleared.' Whether we have that cleaner, better, stronger land is debatable in light of recent events in Germany and the shadow of war hangs over us all again.

I get ahead of myself once more. His Last Bow was published in 1917 and at that time I tried to obtain information regarding what happened to Von Bork after his arrest. Holmes, at the time, intimated that Von Bork would be released in due course and may even undertake ambassadorial duties. I did not think this very likely, one doubts that any country having uncovered a spy in their midst would do anything other than incarcerate him or sentence him to death. When I asked these questions in 1917, I was met with silence. Well, I say silence, but Mycroft communicated with me only to suggest that I kindly drop the matter. Holmes himself was unwilling to discuss the matter with me so I pressed ahead with the story and presented it as I knew it at the time. I believe, however, that Von Bork never made it back to his homeland and met his death on these shores, possibly by firing squad at the Tower of London.

Shortly after these events in 1914, very shortly as it happened, I applied, with Beatrice's blessing, to re-join my old regiment if they would take an aging doctor such as myself. Which, to my surprise they did. To clarify, this was the Northumberland Fusiliers not the Berkshires whom I was attached to at Kandahar. There was little time for training either for the medical staff or the soldiers resulting in a constant stream of battalions and divisions crossing the channel. I was given the rank of captain and assigned duties as a medical officer at various aid posts. I had initially volunteered for frontline duties. I am not sure why, I had no wish to see the fighting that closely, but I did want to get wounded men away from the line as quickly as possible.

Our first real action was at Ypres in late October as part of the British Expeditionary Force. The Germans were desperate to break through our lines to control the ports behind us thereby giving them access to the North Sea. Offensive after offensive followed in which not an inch was given without someone shedding blood. It was wholesale slaughter on an unbelievable scale. I commanded a B section of the Royal Army Medical Corps within the Fusiliers. This comprised, when full strength which was a rarity, one sergeant, one corporal, two privates who acted as wagon orderlies, thirty-six privates who acted as stretcher bearers, one major, captain or lieutenant in command of tent subsection, one quartermaster, one sergeant-major, four sergeants, two corporals, thirteen privates, including a cook, a washer-man and two orderlies. Within days of the battle beginning, we had lost fourteen stretcher bearers and a sergeant.

The action at Ypres[45], just in the first few days, created thousands of casualties. New weapons such as the machine gun caused unprecedented damage to soldiers' bodies. This presented new challenges to doctors and medical staff as they sought to save their patients' lives and limit the harm to their bodies. New types of treatment, organisation and medical technologies were developed to reduce the numbers of deaths.

It was our job on the front line to treat the walking wounded, and this while under constant fire ourselves, and remove the more seriously wounded to a dressing station and from there to casualty-clearing stations for onward movement to base hospitals. Where soldiers ended up depended largely on the severity of their wounds. Owing to the number of wounded, hospitals were set up in any available buildings, such as abandoned chateaux in France.

Often casualty-clearing stations were set up in tents. Surgery was often performed at the CCS; arms and legs were amputated and wounds were operated on. As the battlefield

---

[45] Ypres, is a town in the Belgian province of West Flanders. It's surrounded by the Ypres Salient battlefields, where many cemeteries, memorials and war museums honour the battles that unfolded in this area during World War I.

became static and trench warfare set in, the CCS became more permanent, with better facilities for surgery and accommodation for female nurses, which was situated far away from the male patients. Infection was a serious complication for the wounded. We used all the chemical weaponry in our somewhat meagre arsenal to prevent infection. As we had no antibiotics or sulphonamides, a number of alternative methods were employed. The practice of 'debridement' – whereby the tissue around the wound was cut away and the wound sealed – was a common way to prevent infection. Carbolic lotion was used to wash wounds, which were then wrapped in gauze soaked in the same solution. Other wounds were bipped. That is to say, that bismuth iodoform paraffin paste was smeared over severe wounds to prevent infection.

The experience of life in the lines could be overwhelming. Men were living outside for days or weeks on end, with limited shelter from cold, wind, rain and snow in the winter or from the heat and sun in summer. Artillery destroyed the familiar landscape, reducing trees and buildings to desolate rubble and churning up endless mud in some areas. The incredible noise of artillery and machine gun fire, both enemy and friendly, was often incessant.

It's hard to put into words what this noise did to the men. It was impossible to block it out, I am surprised any of us ever slept. When I slept, I dreamt of the noise of battle, the cries and screams of the wounded and the dying. Yet soldiers spent a great deal of time waiting around, and in some quiet sectors there was little real fighting and a kind of informal truce could develop between the two sides.

Even in more active parts of the front, the fighting was rarely continuous and boredom was common among troops, with little of the heroism and excitement many had imagined before the war.

Sometimes, a new order to go on the offensive galvanised the men to such an extent that cheers would break out in the trenches in spite of the fact that death might be only minutes away. By November and the onset of even worse weather things quietened down for a while. This was in no small part due to sheer exhaustion on both sides. We had pummelled ourselves to a standstill. But there was one final attempt by the Germans to break through.

The main German threat on 11th November would come from two fresh divisions, the 4th Divison and the Prussian Guards. These two divisions, with 10,000 men in twelve fresh battalions, would attack eleven tired British battalions, reduced in strength to around 4,000 men after three months of fighting, along the line of the Menin road.

The German attack was preceded by one of the heaviest artillery bombardments yet, lasting from 6:30 to 9 a.m. Along much of the line the advancing German troops were further protected by early morning mist, but the attacking troops had already lost their early enthusiasm and the attack was turned back by the accurate British rifle fire. The Germans were then pushed back into Nonne Boschen woods and a period of calm returned.

There were a few sporadic attacks after that, but essentially the danger was over. For now. It was a time to regroup, assess our strength or lack of it.

It was a time of fleeting friendships, there was no guarantee that a man you befriended one day would be there the next. Everyone was aware that the next bullet or whizzbang could have your name on it. Life expectancy in the front line was minimal yet the fortitude and good humour

I saw amongst the men was a great testimony as to their spirit. There they were being gassed, shot at, shelled, in the most horrendous conditions yet they sang and laughed their way through it as though they were visiting a holiday camp. Deep down of course they were scared, petrified and homesick for loved ones they might never see again. And now the bastard diplomats talk of war again. It is obscene.

Mr. Huntley, you may wish to edit that particular word out, if I knew how I would, but the whole move towards war makes me heartily sick, hence my language. Have we not seen destruction enough?

To preserve my sanity, I composed letter after letter to Beatrice who now had the added worry of knowing Nathaniel was now in France serving with the Dorset Regiment[46] along with Godfrey Jacob's two sons. Somewhere too, was my nephew I surmised, serving still with the Border Regiment.

It was with a heavy heart I realised that the chances of all of us coming through this hell unscathed was very thin. At this time while there was a bit of a lull on the front line, I was attached to the staff at the nearest casualty-clearing station. The one I found myself in was one of the larger ones and we had upwards of one thousand patients when I arrived, many as you may imagine, seriously wounded indeed.

Some were quickly established as 'Blighty cases' who would be taken, usually by train, to a base hospital near the coast and from there, back home. All too often, after treatment, they found themselves back at the front where they would be extremely fortunate to survive a second time.

Two months into 1915 I was on the move again, this time north towards Lille. There was to be a major offensive with the plan to capture the high ground of Aubers Ridge[47].

---

[46]The Dorset Regiment was a line infantry regiment of the British Army in existence from 1881 to 1958, being the county regiment of Dorset. Until 1951, it was formally called the Dorsetshire Regiment, although usually known as "The Dorsets".

[47]The battle of Aubers Ridge fits the popular image of a First World War battle better than most. The British troops went over the top early

Our section was short on everything including men. On the tenth of March the battle which came to be known as Neuve-Chappelle began. At seven-thirty in the morning the artillery bombardment commenced, and never in all of history had there been such a one. You couldn't hear yourself speak for the noise. It was a continual rattle and roar.

We lay very low in our medical trench just behind the front line, as several of the British guns were firing short. The early success of taking the village of Neuve-Chappelle was soon muted by the stalemate which followed. It did not seem like any kind of victory to us with over 11,000 men perishing and thousands upon thousands suffering grievous wounds. Neuve-Chapelle was the first planned wholly British offensive of the war. It demonstrated that it was quite possible to break *into* the enemy positions, but also showed that this kind of success was not easily turned into breaking *through* them.

I suppose I got used to the conditions we had to work in, the blood, gore and pitiful cries of the men accompanied me in both my waking moments and my sleep. The nightmares began around then and still persist to this day. On the last day of the battle, although we did not recognise it as such then, the casualties were even higher than we had come to expect. The injuries ranged from mere scratches to the most horrific where limbs had been blown away leaving men to bleed to death where they lay. The stretcher bearers were magnificent, retrieving the wounded under such terrible conditions. Their bravery was inspiring. A quick glance at

---

on the morning of 9th May and were cut down by German machine gun fire. The survivors were pinned down in no man's land. No significant progress was made, and early on 10th May Haig ended the offensive. The British suffered 11,000 casualties in one day of fighting on a narrow front.

each man was enough to tell me whether they would live or not. I had words of comfort for each and every one.

One man that day was near to death as I spoke to him. With a struggle he lifted his head and whispered, 'It's Doctor Watson. My God, a friendly face.' Blood and mud covered his face, but recognition came to me. It was Cecil Jacobs. 'Rest easy now, Cecil. Don't try to speak if it pains you.' 'I have to. My brother is out there somewhere. Out…there.' I immediately thought of Nathaniel, was he out there somewhere too?' I gripped Cecil's hand and urged him not to worry about his brother and that I would do all I could to keep Arthur safe. He lifted his head again and made as if to speak, his grip on my hand suddenly tightened then relaxed and he slipped away.

My poor friend, Godfrey, I would have to write to him with the news myself rather than entrust it to the chaplain or commanding officer. First, I needed to find out what, if anything, had happened to Arthur. I questioned soldier after soldier until I pieced together some sort of coherent narrative. He had last been seen leading an assault on a German machine-gun post, leading from the front. None of the party that made up that group had materialised since.

It was possible that they had been taken prisoner, but more likely that they had perished in their brave action. Many years later it was learned that none had been taken prisoner and somewhere in that field there they lie still until such time as they may be discovered, perhaps by a local farmer. No one that I quizzed knew the name of Nathaniel Heidler which was some form of relief at least. As it turned out, Nathaniel, in 1916 was wounded at Verdun, mentioned in dispatches and invalided home. He found life difficult after life in the trenches which is probably an understatement for so many hundreds of thousands would had an equally torrid time in adjusting to a civilian life where everything had changed irrevocably.

In a bid to alter the course of his life, he took over the running of a farm near High Wycombe along with Elizabeth and Rose. They live there still. Constable John Legg, who was such a popular policeman in Lyme, died at Amiens in August 1918. Godfrey Jacobs himself was a broken man after losing his sons and did not long survive them; he died of a heart attack whilst out fishing in 1919.

Sarah Jacobs joined the VAD at the outbreak of the war and served in hospitals on the south coast. Her grief was profound and in 1920 set up a women's charity group in Dorset which she runs to this day. My time at the front was coming to an end. After Neuve-Chappelle I was sent to the No 40 Stationary Hospital in Harfleur[48]. If wounds inflicted by machine-gun fire can ever be called slight, then that is the kind of wound we treated. Many who were seriously wounded did not survive the journey to the base hospital and those who did tended to be shipped straight home on one of the hospital ships which were a permanent fixture in the harbour.

In Harfleur, a nurse caught my eye and I had the feeling I had met her before, but with no idea where and when such a meeting had taken place. During a quiet moment, she sought me out. 'It's Uncle John, isn't it?' 'My word, Charlotte! You were tiny when I saw you last. How on earth did you know it was me?' 'My mother has a photograph of you on the mantlepiece.'

She told me her mother was well and had, at long last married again. He was a fine man, she assured me. Of course,

---

[48]Harfleur is a commune in the Seine-Maritime department in the Normandy region of northern France. It was the principal seaport in north-western France for six centuries

I was pleased that Lily had found happiness and asked Charlotte to send her my love. I asked how James was. Had she heard from him? At this point she broke down and sobbed uncontrollably. James, she told me, had died at Gallipoli where so much of his regiment suffered enormously.

War, bloody war, shattering families, shattering lives. Having obtained Lily's address from Charlotte, I wrote to her offering my condolences and assuring her that I would always be on hand to help in any way I could. Did I really mean that I asked myself? Yes, I did. Time had gone some way to healing the old wounds. I worked with Charlotte for a few weeks until I received further orders that I was to report to the military hospital at Netley as soon as possible. Netley!

I imagined I had seen the last of the place, but once more it was looming large in my life. I left Harfleur on the hospital ship, SS Glenart Castle[49] which was to be tragically torpedoed three years later. I promised Charlotte we would keep in touch and looked gratefully towards England.

---

[49]On 26th February 1918, she was torpedoed and sunk by the German submarine UC-56, ten miles West of Lundy Island, on a voyage from Newport to Brest, to collect wounded. Captain Burt and 94 of her crew were among the 153 killed out of her complement of 186.

Cylinder 11

We steamed into Portsmouth on a day of unbroken sunshine. Never was I so glad to see England. I was relieved to be home, away from the death and destruction I had left behind which would always be with me though. The people of Portsmouth always turned out in thousands to cheer the returning wounded. It was a heart-warming sight that moved me to tears.

And there I was once again at Netley. I barely got settled into my duties when I managed to hurl myself down a flight of stairs. The broken leg I suffered, yes THAT leg, meant that my Army career was over for good. I was not in any way displeased other than the fact I would no longer be in a position to lend support close at hand to our troops, but truth be told I had seen too much death, too much suffering, enough in fact to last me a lifetime. Such was the scarcity of medical staff on the frontline, I had only managed to obtain leave once and had spent a happy, but busy two weeks with Beatrice. Busy because the sale of the Queen Anne Street had now gone through after one or two hitches and our priority was now to find a place to live.

With Nathaniel being invalided home, naturally Beatrice's thoughts turned to her son and daughter-in-law, Elizabeth. Consequently, we bought a small villa on the Sidmouth Road in Lyme Regis and settled to down to a life of retirement amongst those good Dorset folk. Nathaniel had suffered grievous physical and mental wounds and was almost unrecognisable from the man I had known for so long, the irrepressibly cheerful, hard-working provider for his family. He remained in the shadows, in a dark shell which covered him completely at times. It was pitiful to see how far a man can fall through no fault of his own.

He was not alone of course; there were men who suffered as he did, many thousands of men the length and breadth of the country, their lives forever broken. It took time for Nathaniel to recover, but recover he did, albeit not fully. He came to the decision, made jointly with Elizabeth I should say, to radically alter his and their life together. He announced that he had applied for the position of running a farm near High Wycombe [50] in the lovely Chilterns [51] countryside. It would be a hard life he reckoned, but he saw it as his salvation, the chance to start again. Perhaps somewhere the horrors of war would not follow.

For us, a change came too. In spite of our love for Lyme, Beatrice felt somewhat adrift without her family there and we made plans to return to London. It was exceedingly sad to leave Lyme, but there were further holidays to come in

---

[50]High Wycombe is an English town northwest of London. It's in the rolling countryside of the Chiltern Hills.

[51]The Chiltern Hills form a chalk escarpment in South East England. They are known locally as "the Chilterns". A large portion of the hills was designated officially as an Area of Outstanding Natural Beauty in 1965.

that beautiful town. We had no wish to make our home in the city itself. The hustle and bustle of the city which once entranced me no longer offered me anything.

After much discussion and many wearisome house viewings we settled on a property in East Molesey, a three-storey dwelling with a garden which ran down to the Thames. The location was ideal for us with every amenity on the doorstep, including a very fine public house and a cricket ground. What man could ask for more! Other than a few good years to enjoy them. Not that I considered myself decrepit, I was only sixty-six. Certainly, a different story now!

I suppose it is fair to say I was as content as I had ever been. I spent my mornings in writing up various cases I had been involved in with Holmes as my publisher assured me that there was still a market for my humble offerings. Not just a market it seemed, but a growing market. As for Holmes himself? He was still down there in Sussex tending his bees and fending off all attempts to involve him in any form of detective work.

We paid occasional visits to Fulworth and if he came to town, which was a rarity, he would dine with us. We spent our time in reminiscing as old men do with Holmes often forgetting my stellar contributions to our partnership. For us there was no longer the excitement of the chase, but we had a friendship that was possibly stronger than it had ever been.

Beatrice suggested that we got on much better simply because we no longer spent that much time together. She may have had a point. For years to come nothing disturbed the fabric of our lives. We lived a comfortable, happy life. We took holidays when and wherever we liked. I am confident that the listener, sorry, reader will not have any interest in such domestic bliss and time spent together on the continent sightseeing as though our very lives depended on it.

I am none too sure what I have dictated so far fits with Mr. Huntley's brief. I have followed his guidelines in that I have detailed the major events in my life leaving out what some may see as the rather more mundane aspects of life. As the 1920s progressed I had intermittent contact with Charlotte who had returned to Carlisle to be closer to her mother. Lily herself wrote occasionally and I was always glad to receive letters from her. The past, our past, had been put well and truly behind us.

I was still involved in making sense of all the notes I had made of cases that Holmes and I had looked into. Over the years, in spite of periodical attempts to force some kind of order on my detritus of crimes and whimsies barely remembered, no structure had revealed itself. Bearing this in mind and being determined to get, if nothing else, these chronicles in a chronological sequence I purchased three filing cabinets and shut myself away in my study to take matters in hand. I emerged victoriously several hours later feeling inordinately proud of my organisational achievement. It therefore became so much easier to select the next few adventures for publication.

These tales eventually became The Casebook of Sherlock Holmes. I made the decision then, this was in 1927, that this would be the last collection I would bring before the public for I was conscious of repeating myself fearful of my writing becoming jaded I opted to bring matters to an end. I apprised Holmes by letter of my decision and as I expected, he fully concurred. Some of these records still sit here in the filing cabinets, others particularly those I feel are of national importance or simply tales that should never see the light of day have been placed in my old, battered dispatch-box and currently reside in the vaults of my bank, Cox&Co.

Somehow, I or I should say we tumbled into the thirties transfixed by the rush of new inventions, by the sheer pace of change in every facet of life. What a revelation to go and see our first talking-picture! Life was so dramatically different from just forty years ago. Beatrice was prone to labelling me a dinosaur, unwilling to move with the times, but I embrace change and was thrilled with how the world continually re-invented itself.

In January of 1932, I received a letter from Charlotte informing me that her mother had fallen badly on ice and had been rushed to the Carlisle Infirmary where she was in a critical condition with a fractured skull. With Beatrice's blessing I made the journey northwards one more time. Memories crowded in on me during that long trip.

My childhood, almost buried now, was brought sharply into focus with the dreadful news about Lily, my Maid Marian of old. Whatever else was going on in my childhood and I could scarcely claim to have had the happiest one ever, I knew I could rely on Lily to lift me up with her playfulness and her silliness. She was always challenging me to climb a tree faster than she or throw a ball further. I invariably failed to measure up to her prowess at these activities and many others. I became distressed anew at how future events had torn us apart, but I could not desert her now. The bond between us would always be there, indeed had always been there in spite of all that had passed.

I hailed a cab as soon as I arrived at Carlisle station and was driven at breakneck speed to the infirmary. I threaded my way through the wards, breathing in smells so very familiar to me. Turning left into the corridor that would take me to ward eight, I saw Charlotte framed in the doorway, her head bowed. Damn, I knew at that moment I was too late. 'I am so sorry, Uncle. The head injury was too severe,' she sobbed. 'If she had lived she would never have been the same and she would have hated that.' 'Perhaps, all things considered, it is a blessing that she didn't pull through. Charlotte, I cannot even begin to express how I feel. I have known Lily for sixty-six years, it's hard to take in that she has gone. You poor girl, Charlotte.' Lily's husband, Peter, his face tear-stained came to shake my hand. 'She spoke about you often, Doctor Watson. Thank you for coming.'

I stayed in Carlisle until Lily had been laid to rest and made my way back to London, still in a state of shock. One of the perils of getting older is losing loved ones, it is I suppose the natural way of things. Towards the end of 1932, I paid Holmes my annual visit for that is what they had become.

Advancing years meant that I no longer took any delight in the two train journeys, the one by bus and a further one by taxi-cab to Holmes's villa, scenic as they may have been. I was shocked on this occasion by how he had aged, this most indestructible of men. Of course, we were both approaching our eighties, but he had never really shown the ravages of age as I had. That he was ill, was readily apparent to me, but questioning on him brought no results, nor would he allow me to examine him. 'It's nothing, Watson other than a lifetime of bad habits making their presence felt.' 'Well, I was always of the opinion that you pushed your mind and body far too hard,' I responded. 'As to that, my old friend, my state of torpor since the affair you chronicled as 'His Last Bow' should certainly counter-balance to some extent my previous exertions.' Beatrice interjected by saying how we had both come to the conclusion that Holmes would outlive everyone. Holmes threw his head back and laughed long and loud, but it seemed to be a hollow laugh, a laugh of resignation.

I gently probed Holmes on whether he had seen his own physician recently. He resisted all attempts to engage in such a conversation, merely reiterating that he was as well as anyone his age could rightly expect to be. Beatrice suggested we take a short stroll while she tidied up. Holmes's housekeeper, a Mrs. Filbert, for Mrs. Hudson had retired some years previously, had already done a splendid job of cleaning up and Beatrice's suggestion was simply a ruse. Even after knowing Holmes for thirty-six years she imagined that by simply manoeuvring us to be together for a few minutes, he might open up to me. The amble was pleasant. No confidences were forthcoming.

When we took our leave, he shook my hand with such an iron grip it forcibly reminded me of our very first meeting at Barts all those years ago. In spite of his assurances, to me this had all the hallmarks of a final goodbye. I fervently hoped it wasn't so. As soon as were home in East Molesey I penned Holmes a letter, urging him to consult a physician if he had not already done so and if he had done so then to go back for another prognosis. If he wished to avail himself of the very best in medical attention, then I still had some standing in Harley Street circles and I could arrange for someone to motor down and attend him. I imagined my missive, just as my spoken words, had fallen on deaf ears as the weeks went by and no reply was received.

It was to be six weeks before a letter duly arrived. Beatrice had collected the post and handed me the letter excitedly, less so excitedly when she also dropped a couple of bills onto my desk. As I started to read, the colour drained from my face and tears formed in my eyes. I recall Beatrice coming around the desk and have a vague memory of her holding me as I slumped in my chair. The news, especially as it came directly from the pen of Holmes himself was deeply shocking. Not totally unexpected of course. I knew that he was desperately ill whatever his statements to the contrary, but to receive it like this.

But...but...there was a strange comfort in knowing he had reached out to me. I have the letter in the drawer of my desk here. Yes, here it is. It's been quite a while since I have looked at it. Yes, quite a while. It reads:

My dear Watson, my trusted friend and comrade I have painful news for you. News that I suspect will come as no great surprise to you. I observed the look on your face on the occasion of your final visit and knew you feared the worst. Forgive me for not having the courage to tell you to your face that I was living on what is quaintly termed 'borrowed time.'

You may wish to call it an act of cowardice and you may be right, as you often were. The truth is, and perhaps it may be termed an act of selfishness, that I feared to tell you because I would ever reproach myself in my final days for the pain I would cause you and to be constantly reminded of that pain etched on your features would be the source of the greatest sorrow for me. By the time you read these words, I will be no more on this earth. Arrangements have long been put in place whereby my final resting place will remain unknown and unmarked. The scourge of my final years has been the scores of people who desired for whatever reason to seek me out. Some of these misguided souls have attempted to hire my services and involve me in the most trivial, mundane matters you could possibly imagine. Others seemed to be content to gawp at me through the window as if I was a prize specimen in a zoo. I have no wish for my resting place to attract such disparate folk or God forbid, turn my grave into a shrine.

No, I go to my death with as much anonymity as I can muster. My strict instructions to my solicitor also decree there should be no notices of my demise published in any newspaper. I know I can rely on you my old friend to also comply with my wishes in this regard for you have never let me down and have always played the game. I know you will do so this one last time. I think that I may go so far as to say, Watson, that I have not lived wholly in vain, my powers such as they may have been being used on the side of right. Ah, no longer, my innings has been closed to use one of your cricketing terms, Watson. Please convey my regards to the esteemed Mrs Watson, she is in my view and of course I know in yours too, a most remarkable woman. She will be unwavering in her support for you at this difficult time for you. I do not envisage my soul living on through eternity and I know you share my views on life after death. When we die, we die. Please be assured though of my gratitude for your great friendship. You are a man of great integrity and honesty. Should eternity prove to exist then I am, my dear fellow, your friend throughout that eternity. Yours affectionately and in high regard, Sherlock Holmes.

I stared, dumbfounded at the letter, reading it through mechanically time after time. My reaction was one of disbelief, the natural reaction to such news. Shock too and anger. Anger that the essence that made up a man such as Sherlock Holmes would be now crumbling to dust. His exceptional brain, all that knowledge, all those lightning-fast thought processes now lost, gone forever. Unreasonable thoughts maybe as no one can avoid death. It stalks us throughout our lives, taking those we love until finally it calls for us. What was it that…er…was it Samuel Butler said? I think it was Butler. It's gone. Ah, I have it. 'To himself everyone is immortal. He may know that he is going to die, but he can never know he is dead.'

I wanted to tell the world that Holmes was no more, on some level I wanted everyone to know, to share in my loss. Holmes of course had expressly forbidden it and it was far too late in life to rebel against his wishes. Beatrice was unwavering in her love and support. Holmes's death coming so soon after Lily's had dealt me a double-blow of huge proportions. She was ever conscious of my fragile state and allowed me the space I needed. There is a startling identity vacuum that accompanies loss. Those caught in the wake of grief are often swallowed up by feelings of inadequacy, confusion and crumbling self-esteem. I had suffered before from extreme grief and all I can say is that the grief I experienced at Holmes's death was subtly different from that I had known when Mary died.

As before, time heals and a semblance of normality returns. Christmas of 1932 was the ending of that normality. Nathaniel, Elizabeth and Rose descended on us for three days and it was a wonderful festive occasion. We laughed, we sang, we played games. We ate and drank very well, too well, as is often the case at Christmas. On the day they left, the snow began to fall, it was the perfect end to a magical few days. Just a few days later, Beatrice stumbled as she brought in a tray of tea into the parlour. My immediate concern was to ensure that she had not scalded herself, but I was instantly aware that something was terribly wrong.

She stayed in a slumped position, when I asked her how she felt, what had happened, her reply was rendered unintelligible by the slurring of her speech. There was no doubt in my mind that she had suffered a stroke. I made her as comfortable as I could and called an ambulance. She was taken to Kingston hospital. I travelled with her and held her hand and kept talking to her, unaware of whether she could hear me. I urged her to fight hard. By the time we reached the hospital her responses were minimal.

I cannot fault the care she was given, yet after two weeks when you would expect to see signs of recovery, there were none. While there, she suffered two further strokes, neither as severe as the first yet the cumulative effect was crippling. I accepted that Beatrice would not survive although she may live for months, her quality of life would be severely impaired. On one of her better days when she could speak, albeit still slurred, she was adamant that she wanted to come home. I was able to convince her consultant that I would be able to provide the care she needed and it was agreed that Beatrice would be surrendered into my care.

The sadness I felt inside I tried to hide from my features, it would do Beatrice no good at all to see me broken and almost grieving before it was time to do so. Her only sustenance was a little warm tea through a straw. I believe no man could have nursed her better. My resolve and patience were strong, and my love never wavered. She was as beautiful to me as she ever was. She drifted in and out of consciousness, sometimes lucid enough to hold a stilted conversation. During one such conversation she demanded that she be allowed to look into a mirror, to see for herself the extent of her down-turned mouth that now drooped to her left side. She acknowledged her reflection with a simple nod and then turned away. She lingered thus for four weeks.

When the end came it came quickly. Her breathing had become more laboured and shallow. She was awake however and knew I was there, she tightened her grip on my hand. She relaxed a little then and breathing returned to normal. She nodded when I asked her if she could manage a little drink, and I went into the kitchen to prepare some tomato soup. When I came back into the room, I knew she had gone, the whole atmosphere of the room was altered.

But...but...it was the look on her face that astounded and moved me There was a smile, a normal smile, a smile as sweet as I had ever seen. It may be just that the smile appeared due to a relaxing of the facial muscles at the point of death. I have another theory. I think when Beatrice knew she was at that point she put all her conscious effort into creating a smile that she knew I would see when I came back into the room

It was her last act of love. I had suffered with acute grief when Mary died, it was somehow different with the death of

Beatrice. I knew I was strong enough to cope. All the same, it was as though time had stopped, was fractured beyond repair. Without Beatrice, time had shrunk back on itself. Hours, days and weeks merged into each other, all of them empty apart from my memories. The house was silent and fancifully, I thought it missed her. I wandered through the rooms picking up books that Beatrice had read, touched and loved. Her presence was everywhere yet nowhere.

Don't ever believe time heals, it doesn't. It does though, in time, allow one to begin to live again. And now, what of the future? I am eighty-two years of age, I do not know how long I have. I live my life now surrounded by ghosts, I have out lived them all: My brother Henry, Lily, Thurston, Jacobs, my nephew James, Mary, Beatrice. Adeline? She may still live, I have no idea. They exist and live on in my memories of them. Some exist in the memories of others. As for me, who will remember me when I am gone? My publisher assures me that my chronicles of Holmes's cases will always be in print. I am not so sure and besides, is that how I want to be remembered? This has been my life or at least a potted history of the moments and times that meant something to me. I am tempted to follow Holmes's example and die in anonymity, but that may be unfair to Nathaniel, Elizabeth, Rose, Charlotte and anyone else who may wish to mourn me. I have loved and been loved.

I have known extreme joy and seen unspeakable horrors. I have been rewarded with true friendships and a life that had its ups and downs, yet at its best was satisfying. I have tried to do my duty by and to everyone. I am hopeful that my qualities outnumber my flaws. Well, Mr. Huntley, the cylinder is nearly empty and this, for better or worse, is my life.

Acknowledgments:

Thanks to Gill as always for her support.
Thanks too to Steve at MX Publishing for his patience.
Also to Brian Belanger for another great cover.
To Richard Ryan, for valuable advice.
And to Lily Griffiths for allowing me to create the character of Lily Griffiths!

David Ruffle, January 2018

Also from MX Publishing

MX Publishing is the world's largest specialist Sherlock Holmes publisher, with over a hundred titles and fifty authors creating the latest in Sherlock Holmes fiction and non-fiction.

From traditional short stories and novels to travel guides and quiz books, MX Publishing cater for all Holmes fans.

The collection includes leading titles such as *Benedict Cumberbatch In Transition* and *The Norwood Author* which won the 2011 Howlett Award (Sherlock Holmes Book of the Year).

MX Publishing also has one of the largest communities of Holmes fans on Facebook with regular contributions from dozens of authors.

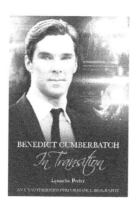

www.mxpublishing.com

Also from MX Publishing

Our bestselling books are our short story collections;

'Lost Stories of Sherlock Holmes' , 'The Outstanding Mysteries of Sherlock Holmes', The Papers of Sherlock Holmes Volume 1 and 2, 'Untold Adventures of Sherlock Holmes' (and the sequel 'Studies in Legacy) and 'Sherlock Holmes in Pursuit', 'The Cotswold Werewolf and Other Stories of Sherlock Holmes' – and many more......

www.mxpublishing.com

Also from MX Publishing

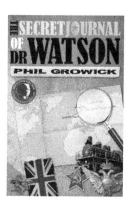

"Phil Growick's, 'The Secret Journal of Dr Watson', is an adventure which takes place in the latter part of Holmes and Watson's lives. They are entrusted by HM Government (although not officially) and the King no less to undertake a rescue mission to save the Romanovs, Russia's Royal family from a grisly end at the hand of the Bolsheviks. There is a wealth of detail in the story but not so much as would detract us from the enjoyment of the story. Espionage, counter-espionage, the ace of spies himself, double-agents, double-crossers...all these flit across the pages in a realistic and exciting way. All the characters are extremely well-drawn and Mr Growick, most importantly, does not falter with a very good ear for Holmesian dialogue indeed. Highly recommended. A five-star effort."
The Baker Street Society

www.mxpublishing.com

Lightning Source UK Ltd.
Milton Keynes UK
UKHW020640100820
367987UK00018B/1924